WELCOME TO THE FALLEN PARADISE

a novel by Dayne Sherman

WELCOME TO THE FALLEN PARADISE

a novel by Dayne Sherman

MacAdam/Cage

MacAdam/Cage
155 Sansome Street, Suite 550
San Francisco, CA 94104
www.macadamcage.com
Copyright © 2004
ALL RIGHTS RESERVED.

Library of Congress Cataloging-in-Publication Data

Sherman, Dayne.
    Welcome to the fallen paradise / by Dayne Sherman.
        p. cm.
    ISBN 1-931561-73-7 (hardcover : alk. paper)
    1. Land tenure—Fiction. 2. Farm life—Fiction. 3. Vendetta—Fiction.
4. Soldiers—Fiction. I. Title.
    PS3619.H4645W45 2004
    813' .6—dc22

                                                              2004014843

Manufactured in the United States of America.
10 9 8 7 6 5 4 3 2 1

Paperback Edition: October 2005
ISBN: 1-59692-152-8

Book and cover design by Dorothy Carico Smith.
Selections from this novel first appeared in a slightly different form in
Country Roads Magazine and *The Distillery*.

For my wife,
Kristy

and to the memory of
my best teacher,
John V. Coumes
1938–1995

For without are dogs, and sorcerers, and whoremongers, and murderers, and idolaters, and whosoever loveth and maketh a lie.
—The Book of Revelation, 22:15

PROLOGUE

The sky was bold, the sun angry. The shade from the live oak was the only defense from the ten o'clock heat.

My cousin Murphy Jr. was dead again. He'd died at least a half-dozen times before. He'd tried drinking rubbing alcohol for a dull buzz, Valium and Drano for immediate suicide, jumping from a tree into shallow water for a broken neck, riding bulls stoned, even knocking up Tank Johnson's fifteen-year-old daughter. He was saved every time, thanks to fervent prayer and modern medicine. But this one did the trick. Brakes failed on his Mustang convertible one night, coming down too fast over the Mississippi River Bridge in Baton Rouge. He never checked up. Went right underneath the tractor-trailer. Clipped his head from his neck like a shear pin splitting off a boat prop.

There are two hills in Watermelon, Louisiana, and I was standing atop one of them. One hill is for grave diggers, the other hill for Jesus Christ. Watermelon has one blinking light at a crossroads, a road sign on I-12 that says "Packwood Corners–Watermelon," and a Baptist church. The Texaco station is across the interstate at Packwood Corners.

People heading to the Mississippi Gulf Coast stop at the convenience store in Packwood Corners where my mama worked and ask about the melons. Not a watermelon for thirty miles. The ground's too wet and soggy. They'd rot in the fields. But melons used to grow green on those sandy clay hills. The hills are full now. On one hill sits Taylor Hill Cemetery, and on the other hill sits Meat Hill Baptist Church, exactly one mile apart, along the Little Natalbany River. It never seemed right to name a church after meat. They named that hill after a slaughter pen. Should have named it after the Taylors who started Watermelon in 1890. Damn if I know why people do what they do most of the time.

It was 1975, and I was standing under the big cemetery oak tree. Digging. That's what I did every time my kinfolk died. Never did it for hire, just when our kin needed a hole. I dug my first one before I had a razor to shave with, or a hair to whack off my chin. Till I joined the U.S. Army in June of 1977, I dug graves. "Best years of your life," my junior high football coach always said. I take offense to that.

The hills used to grow melons a hundred years back, the only two hills south of Ruthberry in Baxter Parish. The world gets flatter and flatter as you head south to Lake Tickfaw. If Columbus had come to Baxter Parish first, and went down the Little Natalbany, he might have fallen right off the edge, and never discovered nothing other than death.

The pickax was heavy. The pick worked the yellow clay and oak roots. Sometimes you had to get the pick when digging a hole. A pick can do things, I tell you. A mound of dirt grew tall on the back side of the hole.

Uncle Red was in the hole with me. That's all we called it when we were digging, the hole. Never called it a grave, never once. It was a hole in the ground, a hole in God's good earth. McMorris Funeral Home charged two hundred dollars to dig a grave. That's why we were digging our own. Money was tight most of the time.

My uncle worked the shovel like a seven-armed gorilla. He was bigger than me, but not by much. The only one there bigger than me, and I wasn't but sixteen years old. I got his no-neck shoulders, arms like stovepipes. I got his temper. He's the only daddy I've ever known.

He lit a cigarette with a wooden kitchen match. He smoked from a stubby unfiltered Camel. "Go take five, son."

I grunted in agreement and pulled myself out of the dirt, the hole three feet deep and seven feet long. He took the pick and started striking the floor of the hole. Three other men watched, all my uncles, his younger brothers. They stood staring with cans of beer stuck in their hands.

I walked over to the watercooler. The water was cold, and plenty of ice still floated around when I dipped the aluminum cup. I poured the rocky liquid down my throat and felt the metallic taste sting my tongue. I drank man-like, tired, worn out.

Uncle Carlin eased into the hole beside Uncle Red, having already tossed a crushed beer can into the bed of his Ford truck parked just away from the hole on the little cemetery lane. Uncle Red loved Carlin, but didn't trust him, how brothers love brothers sometimes. Uncle Red was big and broad, hard-nosed, serious. Carlin was short and happy, laughing and carrying on most of the day. Carlin was the kind of man who will bleed you from behind with a knife stuck in your back, though. That was the problem. Uncle Red put down the pick. He took a deep drag on the Camel. He smoked. The hole waited for his only son.

I looked above the aluminum water cup and saw a white Ford Fairlane lurching up the gravel road. As it pulled into the pea gravel parking lot at the bottom of the hill, I could see that it was Brother Fred Christmas, the pastor at Meat Hill Baptist Church. He was a tall man, six-three, rawboned, 165 pounds soaking wet, wiry, and wired. He reminded me of a cartoon character on TV that I used to watch named Ichabod Crane. His hair was combed straight back over his head and pasted down with hair spray, just like our preacher at the Fundamental Gospel Church in Packwood Corners, which me and Mama used to attend alone on Sundays. My daddy died in Vietnam when I was four. He's in Taylor Hill Cemetery a few yards from the hole.

Brother Christmas walked up the hill like he meant business, just like a schoolteacher catching some boys throwing rocks at the principal's car.

The men never looked up.

"Morning to you, Murphy." He spoke directly to Uncle Red, his voice scratchy and high. "How y'all doing?" he asked, looking around at the rest of us as if he was sizing up a pack of wild dogs.

Uncle Red squinted and nodded.

"I had need to come out here and talk to you. Can't be no funeral service at the church house tomorrow."

My two uncles had eased their beer cans into the bed of the truck when they saw the preacher coming, to retrieve them later. They stepped closer to the hole and closer to the preacher and stuck their hands in their blue jean pockets, and they both chuckled, sounds barely audible, as if they were holding back a flood of laughs behind tight-skinned faces.

"You don't say," said Uncle Red. He took a drag off the Camel, blew smoke out his nose.

"Murphy, that boy wasn't a member of the church. He wasn't even baptized."

Uncle Red wiped a bead of sweat out the corner of his left eye with his index finger. He blew more smoke. "Boy's dead. He's coming to church in the morning for the service at Meat Hill."

"Nossir. Deacons and me done met on it. Now, I saw Tom McMorris for you and he's going to let us have the chapel at no extra charge, a personal favor to me. We can have it there."

Uncle Red pulled himself up out of the mouth of the hole and sat on the ground, his legs dangling over the edge. Carlin stopped shoveling for the first time since entering the hole, propped himself up by the handle.

Uncle Red stared at the gospel preacher. "The boy's mama wants the service at the church house. She's a member."

"That don't matter. Deacons done said. That boy was drunk on that bridge. It said so in the paper. He was a reckless drunk."

"We having the service at Meat Hill Church, Reverend."

"I'm the pastor. We have it where ever I say. I'm the Man of God here," he said, his hands flailing at his side to make the point. He took two steps closer to the hole.

I don't know how, but Uncle Red jumped up and stepped across the hole on high ground. All at once up in the air, the cigarette tight in his teeth. He popped Brother Christmas in the forehead. It sounded like a limb breaking. The preacher fell backwards into the truck side panel. The blow caused him to go down hard. A knot as big as a green lime rose on his head in an instant. Uncle Red snatched him up by the tie, all the way off the ground by his necktie. The man went limp as a decapitated fish eel, but his eyes were alive with fear.

"Sing 'Amazing Grace,' you son of a bitch. Sing it right now. I said sing that song for us to hear."

"Amazing grace, how sweet the sound," he gagged, turning red in the eyes. He mustered up enough wind to sound out the rest, "that saved a wretch like me." The preacher started to bawl, sobbing uncontrollably as Uncle Red let go of his tie. He fell to the ground.

"You'll sing 'Amazing Grace' at the church house tomorrow morning. You'll sing pretty for the boy's mama. Or you'll pack up and go back to north Louisiana where you come from. By God you'll sing. You hear me? You'll sing that goddamn song nice for his mama."

Uncle Red picked the man up by the collar and squared him and looked him in the eye without speaking. He turned him toward his car and pushed him slightly.

The man wailed all the way down the hill. He was louder than a weanling calf crying for milk. He walked stiff and straight-backed. When he got to the Fairlane, he braced himself against the hood with his left hand and took out a white handkerchief from his back pocket. He wiped his eyes and smeared blood across his face.

No one talked. Uncle Red turned to me. "Break's over. Dig."

I jumped back into the hole with Carlin. And dug.

CHAPTER 1

I thought I was gone forever. Germany, Japan, and Puerto Rico. After twelve years in the Army, I thought I was a career man. I was looking for twenty years, eight more to go. But seven months back, on January 17, 1989, Mama was said to be dying of lung cancer. I was in Stuttgart, Germany, when Aunt Cat called to tell me. She hadn't called a single time in all the years while I was gone, but she called this time.

Aunt Cat was my mama's sister, and my daddy's sister-in-law, my daddy's dead brother's wife, my Uncle Roy's wife. I know that sounds complicated. What isn't complicated about a family?

Anyway, they thought it would turn around, the cancer, that is, but she couldn't get on top of it. The doctors said it didn't look good.

I had been trying to bide my time rather than leaving Germany at once, just holding on to see how serious it was before coming home.

After a few weeks Uncle Red called me himself and said to get the goddamn-it-to-hell home. We had words. I told him that I was the man stuck half a world away, and I'd come home when I was damn well able and ready.

Like I said, it looked promising at first, the radiation treatments and chemicals. Then they realized the cancer had spread throughout her glands. Doctors said she had only weeks to live.

The Red Cross verified Mama's terminal illness and came to my aid. I got time off within a few days of the request. I had a month of leave, but I quickly realized that I might need to hold out a week for her funeral, so I only took three. I didn't want to owe the Army an extra day, to take leave in debt for the next year. So I saved that week. Uncle Red held it against me.

By the time I saw my mama in early February, she was lying flat on her back in a hospital bed at Big Charity in New Orleans. She couldn't really talk, only motion, and half-smile and frown. She could only say simple words like "no," "here," and "uh-huh." The doctors even let her smoke in her room, it was so damned hopeless. I had to open the window and make real sure the oxygen was cut off. I don't smoke, but someone had to light one for her, take a drag to get her started, putting it in her mouth to puff, holding it for her. She couldn't even work a match or a lighter by the time I got home.

You had to wonder what was happening to her mind. She never even called my name. I really don't know if the cause of her speech loss was the painkillers or the pain itself or the insanity of seeing your own body fall into rigor mortis. Mama couldn't say "Jesse" if her life depended on it. That disease of the lungs, invited through thirty years of smoking, racked her head like a goddamned blender turned on high, once it got a hold to it, circling the gray matter around till there wasn't anything left but brain juice.

She was dead on April 3, three months after my birthday on January 6. I was long back in Germany at my post as a supply sergeant, a pissant N.C.O. in an M.P. unit, mostly keeping tabs on weapons, bulletproof vests, other equipment, and whatever else in hell the Army needs to keep that big old ball rolling. I was doing work I'd grown to hate, not that I hated being in Supply, I just hated the human relations part of being a staff sergeant, being accountable daily for a rat hole that was never filled, always something missing, and usually it being requisitioned on the Q.T. by someone higher than a supply sergeant. I inventoried with the best of them, worked pencils down past the nub, but you can't do anything when the men above you have a license to steal. I can tell you, in the years I was there, I lifted but one item, a pair of old-model handcuffs, discards headed to the dumpster by the orders of a captain, not theft at all, just saving something from the garbage dump.

For twelve years I had sent Mama a hundred and fifty dollars a month. That was good enough, but I can only say that I was not there for her illness the way I wanted to be, the way I should have been, the way I was expected to be as an only child. I was there at the beginning, then there for the funeral, which they held three days for me to get home.

Mama was a shell in the dark blue casket at McMorris Funeral Home. She was the size of a low whisper, and no amount of embalming fluid and makeup could hide the decay, how it had leaked every ounce of life from her frail body, the way it dragged her down a slot small and tight at the top end, a slot that could never be filled, how it took her to a very small place inside herself and sank her soul to the grave.

She was buried at Taylor Hill Cemetery beside the alleged remains of my daddy. Right beside his Army-issue white marble grave marker with September 5, 1963, chiseled to tell the day.

It was unnaturally cool for April in south Louisiana, low humidity with the temperature in the fifties. The day we had the service was pretty. The grass was beginning to grow soft underneath my patent leather shoes. I walked behind the pallbearers. I wore my dress greens, starched clothes from the Army. I had stripes and the staff sergeant's insignia on my shoulder. My hair was cut high and tight. I was slim and tall and looked all-Army and shone like a silver dollar in this place of death, a gathering of fifty kinfolk at the graveside, where Nards and Barlows and Carters and Tadlocks came to let the ground claim one of their own.

Uncle Red was stoic. He wouldn't speak to me and I made no effort to speak to him. He stood listening to the sermon with a cigarette cupped in his hand. He was a few yards beyond us leaning against a tree, away from his wife, watching things angrily like he is apt to do.

The new preacher at the Fundamental Gospel Church was about my age, short and sincere-looking. Brother Randy was meaty armed, round shouldered, and looked people in the eye, carrying a frown, not some stupid-ass grin like I was used to seeing on the faces of preachers, whether in Baxter Parish or in the Army, the protestant chaplains. This man didn't grin like it was a freaking circus show. He'd looked after Mama, driving down to New Orleans and stopping by at least once or twice a week the whole time she was down there. No, he wasn't like the Fundamental Gospel Church preachers I knew in Baxter Parish, hard-shell preachers, most of them sent down to Louisiana from a Bible college up in Chattanooga, Tennessee, where the church got started. Brother Randy called me the day my company commander told me of Mama's death.

During the service there was a cold shock in the preacher's voice, a light tremble, as if he would never get used to this, there in front of the gray canvas canopy. I heard the question marks hang in his voice as he proclaimed the message of death and the message of life. I respected that. I respected the question marks floating in the air like Jesus hanging dead on a cross.

I sat under the canopy in a black chair. The preacher read from Psalms, chapter twenty-three, how the shepherd looks after his sheep. I could feel a breeze blowing like ice on the back of my neck. But there was no breeze. I was shaken to the core, and I needed to hear this message in Baxter Parish on a heartless day in April.

*

I knew exactly how I landed in those dress greens, what propelled me to join the military. I was eighteen, a few weeks before high school graduation. It was the first week in May. I was working nights at Moultree's Store, doing my best to hold down a forty-hour week, nights and weekends, and trying to finish school. I hadn't done all of my schoolwork. I was behind in chemistry and Mr. Wilson Jenks let me and a couple of other seniors catch up during his off-hour. Everyone knew that Jenks was a bad alcoholic and used to spend the hour in his office at the agriculture shop getting tight, drinking gin neat from a coffee mug, drinking heavy the last hour of the school day. The teacher drove home drunk from Pickleyville High every day without fail.

I walked over to the classroom a minute or two late, having gone to my truck to get a new can of Skoal—in those days, 1977, it was expected that all white male members of Future Farmers of America would use tobacco at school, discreetly perhaps, but at every chance. The can of snuff safely in my back pocket and a fresh dip in my mouth, I walked over to Building C to do my chemistry project. I needed to complete it in order to finish the course and graduate on time.

When I tried to open the heavy wood door to the classroom, the thing was locked solid from the inside. So I started pounding on it pretty hard, the painted glass jolting in the door frame. Janitor Snoot Varasco walked by, and without saying a word, opened the door with his passkey and kept on walking, never looking inside, as if he was some sort of invisible bellhop.

What happened next was one of the most bizarre events of my life, before or since. The first thing I saw was Ivy Williamson's back. He was standing over Chantelle Weary, a pea-tiny-assed senior black girl. He was an enormous kid that I had played football with, and he had Chantelle's pants pulled down and had his hands jammed into her crotch. I could see that much. She was making sounds like she was crying and I immediately saw that there was something stuck in her mouth. I was amazed that with all the banging I did on the door, Ivy hadn't tried to cover things up, but he never even turned around.

Without really weighing the situation, without even shutting the door behind me, I eased between the rows of chairs and sidled up to the teacher's desk, unobserved by Ivy. With my right hand I scoop-lifted a paperweight from Jenks's desk, a crusted-over brown horseshoe with rust clotted through the nail holes. That very second Ivy saw me. His eyes were red. He hit me in the temple, almost took me down, and I heard him laugh as Chantelle began pulling at her panties. Then Ivy grabbed me in a bear hug, but didn't have my right arm penned. A mistake. He rammed me against a tall lab table, and I heard bones crack and pop. I clubbed the bastard with the horseshoe gripped in my free hand, the first time to make him let go, which he did, his nose spreading into a sprinkle of blood and proud flesh. With the piece of steel I hit him for rage and joy and peace and hope, beating him repeatedly till he melted to the dusty floor no longer able to scream. I probably beat him twenty or thirty licks. I was atop him, still beating him with my left fist and the horseshoe in broad and rounding punches, when Snoot and the principal pried me off of his wet body.

That narrow moment, the second before I was pulled off Ivy Williamson, was the happiest time in my life.

Later, the school nurse wondered out loud, within my hearing, as to how his skull wasn't crushed. I was hauled into the principal's office with each man a-hold of my arms.

"Tadlock, have you gone hot-damn crazy?" Mr. Percivil Herrin asked. A wooden paddle hung from a rack on the wall behind his desk like a deer rifle.

"No."

"Well, I damn well wonder. You've about killed the nigger."

"He was trying to rape Chantelle Weary. She was held down and her mouth shut with a rag when I walked in there. He was molesting her. He hit me and grabbed me first, and—"

The principal cut me off. "But the horseshoe, boy? What the hell? I'll have a half million town niggers in here about this if I ain't careful. Son, they were screwing. They weren't making love, but they were sure enough screwing. You hear? They've been caught before on this campus going at it like yard dogs. It wasn't no kind of molestation, boy. Am I gonna have to call Booger Red about this?"

"No. Ain't necessary."

"I'll be. Ain't necessary. This is the third fight this year, and the only thing that'll save cameras from coming out here is Chantelle telling the truth about him swinging first. Boy, you need some discipline in your life."

"What's that?"

"Exactly. You ever thought of joining the service?"

"Why?"

"To save yourself, son. Save yourself from whatever craziness you got in you. Get yourself away from here for a while. Get some discipline."

"Join the service?" I asked again. I thought about his words. My daddy joined up. I'd always admired him for joining at the start of a war, even though it meant I never really knew him. As easy as that I decided to enlist. Just that quick.

"Yes, and I don't care what branch. Go your ass down to that Bayou Square Mall and join the Army or Air Force or Navy or Marines. Go right now. Go now, boy. Get out of here. You join and I might not need to expel you."

I joined up at the first door I came to, the Army's. A couple weeks later I graduated from high school, ten seats down from Ivy Williamson, who was told he'd be arrested for indecent behavior with a juvenile if he said one word. We were in the same row as Chantelle Weary.

When I left Baxter Parish, I meant to leave for good. I left behind a girlfriend that I'd planned on marrying, left her high and dry, my steady girlfriend of two years, Penny Nesom. I told her I'd come back and marry her after boot camp, but I never even returned her letters. I lost touch on purpose. I hurt her bad. I was trying to get away, to survive, to cut off anything that might tie me down to Packwood Corners.

I've had twelve years to rehash all this. I know why I did what I did. I enlisted in the Army not because I was scared of being expelled or not graduating, but because of the way I felt while beating Ivy Williamson. The way I felt pounding his head wasn't right. It was a feeling of joy when I slammed the iron into human flesh. I knew I was one step away from killing him or someone else and landing myself in jail for the rest of my life. Baxter Parish was like some kind of violent fog I'd come up in, and damned if I wouldn't die trying to fight my way out of it.

CHAPTER 2

Two days after Mama's funeral service, before I left for Germany again, a couple of occurrences changed the course of my life. I was actually staying alone at her house, the rent house owned and lent to her for nearly nothing by Uncle Red and Aunt Latrice.

The phone on the wall rang. It was Fred Christmas, the preacher who sang pretty at my cousin Murphy Jr.'s funeral, the day after Uncle Red beat the dogshit out of him in the graveyard. As the story was relayed to me, Old Christmas later took up with the community whore and was defrocked from the Baptist ministry about the time I entered the service. Christmas said on the phone that he was a full-time insurance salesman with New York Life, and he offered his "sincere and heartfelt condolences." Then he dropped his voice down two notches quieter like he was about to offer me a little sweet secret. Mama had made me the beneficiary of a life insurance policy, some thirty thousand dollars tax-free.

I was surprised as all hell. Mama never had two dollars to rub together. Christmas said that she purchased the policy from him in November 1977, and paid the premiums ever since without fail.

I had a hard time believing him till the next day, when he brought me some paperwork to sign at Mama's house and said he'd have the check wired to Germany in two weeks, or deposited into an account of my choosing locally.

But that wasn't the only thing that pushed me into a brand-new world. It wasn't the only thing that helped me decide to leave the Army for good. Fortunately, my contract hadn't ever been signed for another three-year stint. The other thing happened first, actually, prior to the funeral. It was Haltom Roberts talking to me, long-time sheriff of the parish and a friend of the family. During the wake the night before we buried Mama, Sheriff Roberts sought me out and told me he wanted me to come work for him before he left office. He said that he was nearing retirement and wanted to leave the department in good shape for the next sheriff to take over. My military background would be a real plus. He needed someone to run the Maintenance and Supply Barn for the Sheriff's Office; the employees wouldn't get off their asses if an airplane was dropping gold bricks out the sky like raining fish, they were so damned lazy, he said.

I let him know this was a stroke of good fortune, as I could leave the Army soon enough, within a month, an honorable discharge ahead. The sheriff asked me to come see him. He said I'd have a job as a deputy sheriff: logistics manager, as he called the position.

A few hours after Christmas brought over the paperwork for me to sign, the third big thing happened. It was more of a surprise than Fred Christmas calling with the news of a mighty financial windfall or Haltom Roberts asking me to come to work. I was at Mama's house sitting in her stuffed chair reading *The Civil War in Louisiana*, a high school graduation gift from my first cousin Sid Brady, retired history teacher at Baxter State Junior College in Pickleyville. I'd never read this book, but I had read plenty of others while I was away in the Army. My only real pastime while I was gone was reading history. Anyway, I was turning the pages slowly, trying to piece together the story, reading about the fall of the city of New Orleans in 1862, when Johnny, Mama's nub-tailed crossbred beagle hound, erupted into a barking fit.

I heard a car door close. I shut the book and got up to glance out the window.

I hushed Johnny. I saw a woman get out of a blue Toyota car, a tall woman with deep brown hair in a ponytail. She was carrying a basket wrapped in cellophane. It was Penny Nesom and my eyes stung and my throat got as tight as an oil drum and I just stood there gawking at her as she walked to the door.

Before she could knock I opened the door and she stood there with the basket in her hands. Neither of us spoke and there was a silence lasting a moment or two. I guess we were both trying to sort through the last twelve years before speaking.

"I'm sorry about Mrs. Helen. I'm so very sorry. I wanted to bring you some oatmeal cookies and fruit and offer my condolences."

"Penny?" I don't know why I said that. It sounded like a question, like I was unsure who she was, like I somehow forgot her over time, or that she changed so much I really couldn't make out her face. I had not shaved in two days and I was wearing a loose T-shirt and a pair of jeans. I probably wasn't presentable, even though I dealt with Fred Christmas already that morning.

"Yes, Jesse. It's me."

"I know who you are. Come on in. Please come have a glass of sweet tea. I'll make coffee."

Penny stepped through the door and we sat at the table. We talked for two hours. She had gone to see Mama several times, first in Pickleyville at the hospital and then down in New Orleans. Penny worked as an emergency room nurse at Ninth Ward Hospital, she said. My mama mentioned her from time to time over the years when I came home, though I had no idea they were close. Penny said they visited about once a month since we broke up in 1977. I was amazed.

She hadn't been able to go to the wake or funeral because of her work, twelve-hour days, but she'd sent cut flowers. Penny was divorced two years, she said, and had no children. After marrying, she moved to Houston, but it didn't last, was doomed from the beginning. She was back and working at Ninth Ward Hospital.

When Penny left Mama's place I hugged her and walked her to her car, took her phone number, and she took my address in Germany. She rubbed on Johnny, long tender strokes down his back while we talked. I believe he would have loaded himself in her car and left out the drive. I told her I wouldn't be staying in the Army, and I swear a woman's face has never turned as clear and bright, almost mirrorlike with glow.

Penny Nesom is the only woman I have ever loved, save kin. She was a girl when I left for the Army, when I broke off our steady high school love. I hadn't seen her in twelve years. But here she was again, and I could hardly believe it.

I had sex with other women while in the Army, whores in Japan and Puerto Rico. Pay-as-you-go plan. Not often and not in quite a while. I screwed these women but had only made love to one, and she dropped back into my line of vision like the brass ring at the end of a very long battle.

I knew this was it. I knew my running away from Baxter Parish was over. I knew I was finished with the Army and finished with the life I lived since June 1, 1977, when I went to Jackson Barracks in New Orleans to be sworn in as property of the United States Army. I was tired of playing a two-bit supply sergeant, and I was leaving all of Uncle Sam's bullshit behind forever. I was damn well going back home for good.

CHAPTER 3

Six weeks passed quickly between Mama's death and my return to Baxter Parish. I simply didn't re-up with the Army, despite last-minute enticements to do so, promises of a good bonus. I boarded a plane from Stuttgart and was out-processed over at Fort Polk, had the last physical exam, was apprised of all the benefits of the Army Reserves, and told of the amount I had waiting in V.E.A.P., a kind of G.I. Bill for college, if I ever wanted to use it.

I was leaving the military, leaving the only full-time job I'd ever had, leaving my post, the men and women I served with, the few friends I made in over a decade of military service. And I felt sadness like I hadn't experienced in a long time, at least not before or since Mama wasted away. I didn't know how leaving a career behind could be so hard on a soul.

Of thirty thousand dollars in Mama's insurance policy, I hadn't spent a dollar. I'd saved seven thousand on my own already, the most I'd ever put up, enough to buy a forest green 1982 Chevrolet pickup, with a little left over to keep me going. All of the policy money was untouched. I bought the Chevy through the Leesville, Louisiana, newspaper. It was a one-owner in good shape, bought just off the base near Toledo Bend. The truck was well kept, owned by an engineer at a power plant. It was a like-new stepside, the best vehicle I ever owned, the 305 engine and automatic transmission able to purr like a milk-fed cat.

I loaded all of my possessions, two duffel bags' worth, my clothes and a few odds and ends I'd shipped back from Germany. Stuffed it all in plastic garbage bags and left it in the bed of the truck for the drive home.

The highway from Fort Polk was flat and long to Lafayette, and I felt unstable on it, the most unsure of myself since I left Baxter Parish for the Army years ago. I thought the service would make me belong, save me from the violence I'd seen, but I had miscalculated. The Army was not a cause to live for, and it wasn't much of a cause to die for either. I found no real brotherhood there. It was a bureaucracy deeply intertwined with the dual thoughts of killing and retirement, those two things, in that order. It was a part of my life that had been spent and was gone, twelve years' worth, and I would soon find additional reasons for living, I hoped. I'd seen the world by some standards, at the cost of not being free to go and come as I pleased. I was only allowed to leave for thirty days a year, to come home and turn around and go back. In the faraway places that I was stationed, getting home was tough to manage, often by design. I would just as soon not face the decay and trouble lurking at home.

I traveled to southeast Louisiana during the day and evening, nonstop driving, except when I needed to piss or buy gas. I ate bologna sandwiches that I'd bought at a gas station and drank coffee out of a stainless steel thermos to stay awake.

It was mid-May, hot on the highway, and I kept the window cracked to circulate the air in the truck, the air conditioner just a cause to burn gas. At least during the night on I-10 it had been cooler than out in the central part of the state. When I crossed the imaginary border into Cajun Country, the sweat on my back finally dried into the cotton of my white T-shirt.

I had time on the road to think about Penny. I was moving from place to place since I last saw her. I never got a letter, but it didn't bother me. I planned on calling her first thing when I got back.

"Enter Baxter Parish," the sign on the interstate read. Enter I did, the second I passed the Little Natalbany, over the concrete bridge at the creek where I spent plenty of time fishing when I was a boy. Reading the sign let me know I was finally home.

As I took the exit off I-12 I could see the highway was lit up near the overpass. I turned at the Packwood Corners–Watermelon exit. When I saw the convenience store where my mama used to work, I wondered how many hours and days and weeks she had spent there, how much of her life was spent watching the business for someone else. The store was closed, dark inside. She'd made night supervisor, working there twenty years.

I knew that some other woman probably took Mama's place already, and this woman would be there at night till closing, a cigarette glowing in the window, night after night, week after week, year after year. When I saw the store I knew much was the same back home, no matter how I hoped inside that life could be different. The store will always be the same.

By my age, thirty, Daddy had been dead seven long years. My mama, by my age, had an eleven-year-old son to care for. At thirty years old she'd already settled into Uncle Red and Aunt Latrice's rent house for the hundred bucks a month that she would pay till her death, fifteen years of renting the house cheap from kin. Now, I would go through her things and stay there till I could find a house of my own, a place bought and paid for by Mama's insurance money.

She always wanted a piece of land, and from the stories I remember hearing, my daddy died hoping he'd have a little land himself. He wanted land of his own and mentioned it when he told Mama good-bye at the bus station in Pickleyville the last time he saw her, when I was three years old.

I had simple plans for the money, to damn well buy myself a place. I'd have something she was never able to enjoy for herself: a house and land registered in our own name at the courthouse in Ruthberry.

The weeks since Mama died gave me a period to reflect, allowed me to wonder about how I should spend my life after the Army. I figured a deputy sheriff's life, not a real deputy sheriff but a logistics manager, wouldn't be a bad one, owning a piece of land and a house free and clear, thanks to the policy. At least I had somewhere to stay for a while till I found what I was looking for, and I had more than thirty thousand dollars in savings at the First Louisiana Bank in downtown Pickleyville to make sure I wouldn't spend all my years renting.

The interstate was at least a couple of football fields wide. I turned down Old Sawmill Road, a country road that wasn't a thoroughfare. It was a two-lane blacktop with no shoulder, winding its way through the piney woods flatscape. The moon lit the pasture on one side of the blacktop; there were shadows in the road from the tall trees that bordered the ditch to the left. I listened to Bruce Springsteen on the radio sing about glory days, his glory days and, I guess, those of every man who has ever lived.

I took a left into the drive at my mama's rent house, Uncle Red's house, a gray cinder block two-bedroom near the street, and I heard the gravel crunch underneath the truck tires as I pulled in. It was here that my mama lived alone while I was away following my own exit plan from Packwood Corners and Baxter Parish.

Mama's old car was parked under the carport, just sitting up unused since her illness, unused except for the few times I drove it while I was home in February and April, when I came back to see her in the hospital and for her funeral. I noticed when I stopped that

Johnny wasn't there. I recalled Aunt Cat took him in when Mama got ill, and except when I came home, he'd been living with her. Johnny would shake his whole ass-end when he greeted you. My mama loved the dog and Johnny loved everybody he sniffed.

When I opened the pickup door there was silence. No bugs, no cricket sounds, just dead quiet in the yard. Not even a car on the highway. It was too far from the interstate to hear the sounds of the big trucks. There was nothing to mark this place as being anywhere, really. It was all by itself, alone.

The next thing I noticed after the lack of noise was the soggy ground under my boots. Mama always hated the frog-pond yard in Packwood Corners, where the water table is close to the topsoil and the land is so flat that rainwater hardly drains.

I went looking for the house key in the dark. The key was left under a plastic flowerpot placed atop a round cedar table on the carport, right near my mama's worn-out car. I opened the door to the house and the damp smell hit me in the face, the house having been shut up for months since Mama was diagnosed. The smell slapped me with such force that I knew it was not just the smell; it was also the indication that she was lost and would not return. Neither time nor memory nor fate itself could restore her. The smells showered the moment with decay. I turned on the porch light at the panel in the kitchen and then flipped the switch to the light over the dinner table and walked through the door, back outside. I'd left my bags in the truck. Once inside the house again, I took off my shoes and went to sleep on the couch immediately with all of my clothes on, including a worn Atlanta Braves baseball cap on my head.

The next morning I drove a mile and a half over to Aunt Cat's house on Delmar Road. She lived alone, a widow. Uncle Roy died when I was twelve years old. Aunt Cat was like a second mom to me, as she and Uncle Roy never had any children of their own.

I knew that she would have biscuits cooked, the woman aware that I was coming home. I wasn't through the door good when she hugged me, the smell of biscuits and coffee and cigarette smoke surrounding her like a nostalgic shadow.

"Jesse," she said, "it's fine having you back. So good to have you safe. Latrice and Murphy have missed you, too." She had changed little since I left in 1977. Her features were square, the edges of her face lean. She looked a lot like Mama.

"Uncle Red wasn't all that friendly when I came back home for the funeral. He never said a word to me."

"It's his way. He knew you were stuck in the Army while she was sick. We did right by her, and there wasn't nothing you could do and he sees that. You know how he feels about the Army."

"About the same as I do now." I knew what he thought about the military. He lost two brothers to war and he barely made it home himself. His war was Korea, and his brothers—Uncle Tom Ed and my daddy, Ernest—died a few days apart in Vietnam. Uncle Red all but begged me not to go once he'd found out, but I'd already signed the papers. He never knew why I was leaving, about the escape route from the parish. He wanted me to go to the junior college, Baxter State, and offered more than once to pay my way the whole time I was in my senior year. I joined anyway in spite of this and stayed in the Army for a long time, longer than needed. What he didn't know was that Mama asked me to stay put in the Army. She didn't want me to be a part of a dead-end place, a place filled with death and violence, a territory sunk in the mire of unemployment and poverty. She said I had a chance of making it in the Army, at least when we were not at war. Even while she was sick, she asked me to stay in Germany.

"Where's he gone to?" I asked, having passed Uncle Red's house on the way over, seeing that his pickup was gone.

"Latrice called this morning and said he was fishing Lake Tickfaw alone. The plant laid him off two weeks ago and he's drawing unemployment, fishing and thinking of doing a lot more of it for cash money, she said. At least it'll make a little extra money until he hears from the union hall about another job. Can't say getting him out of the house is bad either, from what Latrice says." Aunt Cat lit a Pall Mall with a white-tipped match, placing her red pack on the aluminum table. She motioned for me to sit down. "She says he wants you to start running crab traps with him. She told me last week."

The thought rolled around in my head a minute. I wanted stable employment. I'd heard the horror stories of how the Louisiana oil bust was still destroying the state, the lack of jobs worse than during the Great Depression, and how scores of natives left to find work elsewhere. "Well, you know I'm going to work with the Sheriff's Office, but I reckon there'll be time enough for fishing."

"You could fish on the side," she said.

"Maybe so." I remembered how Uncle Red and his son, Murphy Jr., used to fish together all the time, till about age fifteen, when Murphy Jr. began to like drinking beer and smoking dope a hell of a lot more than fishing. A question remained in my mind whether he purposefully killed himself crossing the bridge, a suicide. I know others questioned the way it all happened, too, but we pretty much kept quiet about it for Aunt Latrice and Uncle Red's sake.

Aunt Cat passed me a plate of warm biscuits covered by a green dish towel. The biscuits were broken apart in the middle and already buttered. They were soft and tender, kind of small with a light dusting of flour on the outside. I smeared homemade strawberry jelly on a couple of them and enjoyed the cup of coffee she'd brought to me in a heavy mug.

When I stepped out the house after I finished eating, Mama's dog wandered up and greeted me with the welcome of his paw on my shin. Then Johnny started bouncing in circles, his legs like coil springs and his nub tail wagging.

"How are you feller?" I reached down and patted the dog on his meaty head and pulled at his long ears. He stopped and took in all of the attention. I pulled the skin on his ear between my fingers and he looked down in pleasure and I squatted and rubbed him more. During the small bits of time when I came home on leave, the dog would take to me like I was his sole master, and after I left, Mama would write me letters telling me that the dog grieved a week when I returned to the service. Johnny was the only dog she'd ever let stay in the house with her.

"Boy," I said to the dog, "you want to come home?" I went back inside and let Aunt Cat know that I would be taking him with me.

Aunt Cat wanted to help me clear out Mama's stuff, so we rode to the house in my truck with Johnny in the bed. I sure let her help. She worked like a buzzing bee. Watching her work made me wish Penny was there to help as well.

The remainder of the afternoon we cleaned up around the house. As soon as I took Aunt Cat back home and returned to Mama's, I slept till it was dark.

Over the years I dreamed about Penny, dreams at night and daydreams. I guess I'd seen her face daily, sometimes in the face of another woman. I carried her in my mind. It wasn't an obsession, but it was a clear memory, almost a haunting.

The guilt got after me sometimes. It would sting me, just like when I opened the door to her that day. Guilt and regret follow me often. I'd wanted to marry her when I was eighteen, before I panicked and ran away to the Army, scared of falling in love and being a father, scared of what violence might be working itself around in my soul.

As best I knew how, I was trying to get away from the trouble of Baxter Parish. There were the stories and tales of feuding from a century ago and the killings as recent as a week ago, the vigilante justice that marked the region since the Civil War. The night riders who slaughtered people in ambushes on lonely country roads, back when the history books say Baxter Parish had a rural homicide rate higher than anywhere else in America, and was called Bloody Baxter Parish for good reason, for good cause. Uncle Red and his brothers were always in a fight. I guess during the history of the place, Tadlocks were regularly in feuds. I'd seen my share of strife.

Some people believe that when a door shuts another opens. They mean everything is getting better, that God is looking after us. I have a hard time with that one. I don't rightly believe that everything happens for a reason. It doesn't happen for a reason, save the wonder of gravity, the chain of events. You drop a rock and it falls to the ground. That's the law of nature. You pick up the same stone and throw it at a man and hit him in the forehead, he dies. That's the law of nature too. For the most part, one door does lead to another like a chain reaction, but the next door might be a bitter end. I just don't believe all things work together for good.

For my part, I left Baxter Parish to try to stop fate, but now at this time in my life I had plenty reason to be optimistic in spite of myself and my experiences: the insurance policy, job, and Penny gave me hope that my luck had changed, suddenly, and perhaps for good.

The next morning, I went to the Texaco station where Mama used to work and bought the Sunday edition of the *Pickleyville-Star Register*, and combed the classifieds for a house and land. There was one listing for a rustic cabin and ten acres in "God's Country," the ad said, on the

state line up in Mount Olive at the north end of the parish. I figured it
was far enough away from Packwood Corners to make my new start
complete and fresh. The asking price looked really good, thirty-three
thousand dollars.

Even though it was Sunday, I went on and called Sunnyside
Liquidators, the company up in Ruthberry with the ad in the newspaper. A man answered the phone, a deep-voiced fellow who said to call
him Sam, Sam Bullfinch. He said the office was not open but that the
phone system forwarded the call to his house.

I told him I was interested in the land up in Mount Olive, the
cabin and ten acres listed in the paper. I asked him if it was hilly. He
said that it had rolling hills and was remote, if I liked remote. I said
remote is just fine with me.

He went on to tell me about three other properties in Baxter
Parish, all costing more than fifty grand.

While I talked to the salesman, Johnny was stretched out on the
rug in Mama's living room, his head flat on the floor. The dog's ears
moved in concert with my voice. He was across from where Mama
used to sit in her blue La-Z-Boy chair. I watched him while listening
to Sam talk about the other properties.

"Look," I said, "I'm not interested in paying fifty thousand for anything. I called about the ten acres and cabin."

"Sir, that's not my contract. My partner Jerrod Bass has the one
you're talking about. He's handling it for the bank, a repossession."

"Well, that's the one I'm interested in. Can you sell his stuff?"

"Yeah, I can. Jerrod's out with gallbladder surgery. I usually let him
handle those repos, but I will sell them. I normally sell movable property such as cars and office equipment, anything repossessed or lost in
bankruptcies. My partner takes care of the real property."

"Why don't we set something up so I can see it?" I asked.

"I told you the property is in the middle of nowhere on the state line. Why don't you just take a ride up there? If you're still interested, give me a call."

"OK." I was a little perturbed by his lack of interest. "On second thought, I want you to go up there and show me the property. If you don't want to show it, I'll call Century 21. Can't they sell it?"

"They can, but that won't be necessary. I'll take you," he said, sounding reluctant for some reason. I figured it was the low asking price.

He said that the property was off Highway 38 and that it belonged to Tickfaw State Bank and had an old wood-frame farmhouse on it. It was on Spears Road. I hadn't ventured around up there much and didn't know exactly where it was located.

"I do want to see it," I said.

"See it you will, dear friend," Sam replied.

I mentioned that I had to fill out paperwork at the Sheriff's Office in Ruthberry and that I'd like to go look at it afterward on Monday, maybe four o'clock. He agreed to meet me at his office in Ruthberry, Main Street near the tracks.

I'd already called the Sheriff's Office while I was at Fort Polk and the chief deputy, Felix Dufrene, said for me to be there at one on Monday. Everything seemed fine with the new job.

After the call to Sam Bullfinch, I took a short nap on the couch. It was nine-thirty and Johnny curled up beside me, half on my leg, all twenty pounds of him, and we slept a deep sleep till noon, the deepest kind of sleep that I had known for a long time. When I awoke, I hustled in and out of the shower and got myself dressed. Johnny still lay asleep on the couch, stiff as an oak board.

At twelve-thirty, I rushed over to Aunt Cat's for Sunday lunch, roast with rice and brown gravy, and I visited with Aunt Latrice, who'd come over to eat. Both Aunt Cat and Aunt Latrice acted excited about the land up in Mount Olive. Aunt Latrice said that Uncle Red would be happy about it. He was running fishing lines and could not come.

Would not come, I thought.

After the meal, I drove out to Pickleyville and bought some groceries for the refrigerator, and a few odds and ends to survive civilian life.

On Monday morning I got up late, about ten, and prepared myself for the job interview. I drank plenty of black coffee and I tried to think ahead about what might be asked during the meeting. I later drove out east on I-12 and then north on I-55 to Pickleyville. I stopped at the Hard-Row Barbeque on the way, a squatty brown cinder block building with neon beer signs lit in all of the windows.

The old black woman behind the counter, Celeste, took my order. "Two pork!" she screamed to the cooks behind the thin wall, the sound transmitting through an open window to the back room. She added the total price in her head, including tax, as I stood at the bar.

"You look like a Tadlock."

I smiled in the mirror behind her. "Well, I would be a Tadlock."

"Which'n?"

"Murphy's nephew."

"Your daddy Carlin or the others? Or Roy, the one what's dead?"

"The other one that's dead, Ernest."

"Sorry about your mama passing."

"Thank you."

"You look just like Red. He eats here two, three times a week lately. He eats five beef at a time. Why you trying to be a lightweight?"

"I'm trying to stay lean."

"And mean," she said.

"Uh-huh."

"You still in the Army?"

It surprised me that she would know all of this. She was in a position, however, standing at that bar every day for forty years, to know just about all that happened to folks in the parish. "Not anymore," I said. "I'm trying to get on with Haltom Roberts."

"I'll put in the word if I see the sheriff. You'll make a good one."

"I hope so."

After eating the two sandwiches and drinking a cold root beer, I got back on I-55 and drove toward Ruthberry, twenty miles north, for my appointment to do the paperwork at the Baxter Parish Sheriff's Office. Mount Olive would be another ten miles up 55. At least I was headed in the right direction.

Pines bordered the interstate highway along with cow pastures and ponds dug in the sixties to build overpasses. The engineers needed plenty of dirt to build up the twin highway tracks heading north and south, to keep the interstate from flooding, so there were ponds dug everywhere. The interstate was as flat as a pressed dollar bill, straight and without many curves, just straight as a chalk line.

I saw remnants of farms owned by Italians who had been on the land for a hundred years, growing strawberries and peppers and cabbages along the interstate. In this little world, all you had was flat till about a mile north of Ruthberry, where the hill country begins as if all of those ponds were turned upside down on the way to Mississippi. These were the same hills where Governor Earl K. Long, Huey P.'s younger brother, used to hunt wild hogs and spend time with his dirt farm supporters in the piney woods. When Uncle Earl stumped at election time up and down Old Highway 51, and beat his straw hat across his thigh to make a point, the poor souls knew exactly what he meant, exactly what he was saying.

It was hot on the interstate, hot enough that I was willing to indulge the air conditioner in the truck to keep cool in my dress shirt and slacks while I went to see about the job.

In Ruthberry, the parish seat on Highway 16, they had a new shopping center with a Tidwell's Grocery and some gas stations. Except for these businesses, it was just like when I left, still country, a two-lane blacktop road heading through the heart of the rural Florida Parishes.

When I pulled into the parking lot near the Sheriff's Office, I saw Haltom Roberts getting into his police cruiser on Oak Street right off of Main, right down from the courthouse. Roberts was a short man with stubby arms and a cleft chin, the red look of hypertension in his face. He was a man caught up in turmoil and contradiction, hazards of his work and status in the parish, and it showed in his face. He was cursed with trying to be all things to all men.

"Tadlock," he called out to me. "Go and see Felix in the office." He gave me no greeting. "Let him get you signed up." He hollered it out like a command, his head ducking into the cab of the squad car as he slammed the door shut and pulled out of a reserved parking space.

Roberts was a little younger than Uncle Red. My people had known his people for the longest time. It felt real good to have a job waiting. Seeing him at the funeral home that night made leaving the service seem like a good decision. Having a job and somebody to trust to work for was a real incentive to come home, I figured at the time.

The building was next to the courthouse, and it seemed a crisscross of halls inside. Men and women walked freely throughout unhindered. Even trusties in orange jumpsuits walked around the halls with mops and water-filled buckets cleaning the floors.

I asked the old woman at the receptionist's desk where I could find Felix Dufrene. She pointed around a corner without looking up, her face buried in the weekly newspaper.

Dufrene sat at his desk writing on a yellow piece of paper when I opened his office door.

"You Mr. Dufrene?" I asked.

"Yes sir," he said. "You Mr. Tadlock?"

"Jesse Tadlock." I extended my hand.

"You ready to go to work?"

"I am."

After shaking my hand while seated, he held up two fingers like the sign of victory. "Two weeks to process you. You're military, ain't you?"

"Supply sergeant, twelve years active duty in the Army."

"All you'll need is to get certified on a pistol and do our little Thursday night program for eight weeks and you'll get a take-home car, but you won't be a regular patrol deputy. You'll be more of a supervisor, so you won't have to go to the police academy over in Baton Rouge. You'll get a badge and a car nonetheless, and you'll have full arrest powers, though you won't have to carry a weapon every day."

I sat in a plastic office chair without him inviting me to do so, just sat down after a minute.

He told me about the job, pay, work schedules, expectations, talked aimlessly in circles for an hour. The man talked about his kin down in the south end of the parish. Ronny-Boy Dufrene and all the others in Milltown.

Finally, he sent me across the hall to be processed. A woman deputy, so thick at the waist that her gun belt made her stomach spill over, took my fingerprints. I filled out the paperwork, did the song and dance like I've always done for every new post in the Army. Processing.

Back in Dufrene's office, on the way out, he reassured me of a good take-home car for the third time. Then he grabbed me by the shoulder. "This here is a family, Tadlock. It's a big family, and Haltom Roberts is like the daddy you never knew. I was a friend of Ernest's. I knew Tom Ed. I know they died over in them goddamned rice paddies where we was fighting gooks. Haltom Roberts is your sheriff, see, and he's the daddy to this whole goddamned world in Baxter Parish. He's your boss and he's the law. We're brothers in two weeks' time. You remember that and you'll make twenty years."

My shoulder burned a little when he let go. I felt a tingle and I smelled a thousand cigarettes blow out of his lips, the fire in his face, the smell of dead ashes, the strange scent of deceased words.

The chief deputy smiled at me and opened the door of his office for me to leave.

I went back into the day's heat and opened a hot truck door. I felt sort of uneasy about Felix Dufrene's message. I thought he was being overdramatic, and I didn't know why.

The street was busy with cars and I waited till the traffic slowed to pull out. Just across the tracks, a half mile west, I turned at the first building, the property office that I'd seen on the way into town. There was a sun-yellow sign painted on the front of the brick building; the same yellow sign was spread across a tan Bronco's door in the parking lot, big magnetic signs to grab your attention.

The bells jingled at the glass door, and I felt a drop of sweat slide down my armpit into the skin on my side.

"May I help you?" said the rotund man, maybe forty-five years old. He walked right up to me. "I'm Sam Bullfinch, life member of the Louisiana Liquidators Hall of Fame."

I shook his hand. It was so sweaty I immediately regretted it.

Me and Sam rode together in his Bronco. He talked about every other property for sale but the one we were going to see, and I reasoned that he was just trying to milk me for a bigger commission.

Topography started to change when we left Ruthberry, the change always amazing to me. The hills reminded me of the German country-side. It was a different Baxter Parish from the one down home, thirty minutes to the south. It was beautiful, rolling hills, farm ponds, natural springs in the sides of steep red clay embankments. The country was almost like Appalachia, the hills green and lush with vines.

The old house and land were out east of Mount Olive on Spears Road, which is also called North Factory Road, I learned, a thin stretch of parish road that bordered Walthall County, Mississippi, a road hemmed in by big dairy farms and pine plantations, land that once held cotton fields, and even earlier, virgin longleaf pine.

We pulled onto Spears Road, a solid gravel road, and drove about a mile. There were no houses that I could see out there, just an occasional dirt driveway beside a banged-up mailbox.

Sam stopped his Bronco in the middle of the road, leaving the motor running. "Brother, this is where the parcel starts, and you have six hundred feet of frontage. You go back about seven hundred feet, straight back. You can see that it's got plenty of good trees, pasture and some brush." He pointed to the back of the land.

We drove down an oyster shell and red clay drive, crossing a cattle gap made of pipe, and immediately I saw the house, a wood-frame farmhouse with a pitched tin roof, the kind of house you'd imagine is haunted by the death of an only child. The porch was raised wood, and it went all the way across the front. It wasn't a big house, probably thirty-five by twenty-five.

There were no signs of people there, the yard empty. The house sat atop a small hill with a couple of pecan trees that I noticed right off. There was a big thicket encircling the whole property, and what appeared to be twelve thousand stubby Chinese tallow trees no more than ten feet tall, and some scattered loblolly pines.

Sam crawled out of his Bronco and began pointing again at the house as if I hadn't seen it.

He went up the steps and unlocked the front door with a key from inside a little box hanging on the doorknob. He said the lights had been off for a while and the bank recently paid for the cleanup.

"If you want rural property, this is rural," Bullfinch said. "And if you want a fixer-upper with all kinds of potential, you have it here, brother." The salesman smiled wide.

"What about neighbors?" I asked.

He stalled a second. "There ain't no neighbors. The woman who lived here committed suicide. Now I'm supposed to tell you in case it would be a reason you wouldn't want to buy it. I'm a professional liquidation salesman, and we have a code of ethics. The lady didn't do it here though, not inside the house. The bank took the property to pay off her mortgage. Her family lives nearby, but like I tell people all the time, if you can't see neighbors, you ain't got none."

"They want thirty thousand for the place?" I was thinking how much they might fall off the price.

"Thirty-three's the asking price," he said.

Once inside, I walked down the center hall. I moved my weight up and down on the pinewood floors and they felt real solid. The ceilings were wood, beaded board at least ten feet high.

Paint was peeling inside and it probably needed some electrical work. There weren't any water stains on the ceiling to indicate a bad roof. The hallway was nice, at least six feet wide, and there were four good-sized rooms, all four exactly the same size, and one was the kitchen. The bathroom was scabbed off the side of a bedroom, which made me sure it was added later. The first bathroom must have been an outhouse. A small screened-in porch was attached to the kitchen, and there was a lean-to carport with a concrete slab off the screen porch.

An empty corncrib made of rough-hewn timbers sat in the backyard; it was off the ground a few feet and set on a foundation of heart pine blocks, the blocks shrouded in tin to fight off the rats. Twenty feet away was an old log smokehouse about eight feet by eight, and it housed some odds and ends, a middle buster plow in pretty good shape, the two wings beside the plow point stuck out in an iron V.

After poking around a while, I checked the sills under the house, scooting around beneath the floor joists on my belly where cobwebs and cool dirt made me feel like I'd entered a cave. I prodded the wood with my pocketknife blade to check for rot and termites, and I found none.

There was a tin shed with an electric water pump, and close to the carport was a propane tank painted dull silver that kind of looked like a long-bodied hog foraging for acorns.

Sam and I walked the property lines, and he asked what I thought of the place.

"I'll give them twenty-eight, and I want the septic tank and water well guaranteed to work," I said, looking at him as he leaned against the hood of the Bronco with his elbows bent, his hands clasped like a man in prayer.

He glanced at the wristwatch on his hairy arm. "OK. We'll sign a contract on your offer, but it's too late now to tell the bank. I'll let them know first thing in the morning. I believe they'll take it."

I felt real good all the way back to Ruthberry, the two of us making small talk in the Bronco. It felt good to own what my mama and daddy never owned: a home place. It seemed damned amazing how simple and easy it was to find a good piece of property to buy at a fair price. This would be a place with no mortgage, no one to say it wasn't mine.

Once we got back to the office, Sam gave me a copy of my contract. I was looking forward to telling people that I was moving to

Mount Olive on ten acres and a house, that I had a new job. The only missing part was a woman, and I planned on working hard on Penny to take care of that too.

I called her later that evening from Mama's house, and she said she was happy to hear from me. We chatted for an hour, talked about getting together. They were understaffed at the hospital and she was working extra shifts. I had plenty to talk about, and she said she'd be free to go out in two weeks, that she was stuck working some back-to-back shifts at the hospital, making double-time.

The next day, the salesman phoned at ten. Sam Bullfinch said I'd just bought myself a farm. His tone of voice was somber, and he mentioned again a steal in Liberty City on twenty acres and a brick house. I told him I wasn't interested. He said the name of a mortgage officer at the bank, but I explained again that I wouldn't be borrowing any money. This place, I said, would be owned free and clear. A local title company could work up the papers cheap, and we could close Friday in two weeks, he said. The closing was set for the Friday before I was to start work at the Sheriff's Office.

Coming home to Baxter Parish couldn't have been any better. The reason I came home, my mama's death and the final disillusionment with military bureaucracy, wasn't nearly as important as the fact that I'd made it back home again. Years across the globe meant very little to me. The service was at worst a diversion, and at best a season in time for me to grow up. I was home, by God, and I planned to live in the north end of the same parish of my birth, live out my life with a decent job, work that was needed.

A little less than two weeks later, I signed the papers at the title company in Ruthberry, right across the street from the Baxter Parish

School Board. It was eleven in the morning and I signed the papers without a minute's hesitation or doubt. A train barreled down the Illinois Central Railroad tracks south to New Orleans, and I swear the table vibrated as I sat beside Sam signing the deed.

My pickup was loaded with the furniture I'd taken from Mama's house, a table and four wooden chairs, an ironing board, kitchen items including a small microwave oven. There were towels and sheets for the bed that would need to be hauled during another trip, the truck already packed tight. As I sat with the legal secretary for the title company and Mr. Bullfinch, I couldn't think about anything but that land and the possibilities for the future. How I might plant fig trees and blueberry bushes, and how with a little savings I might even get an old John Deere tractor and try to raise watermelons on the hill just outside the yard near a little dry creek. But my smile didn't look anything like the frown wiped across the face of the salesman sitting at the table. This was hard to read.

"Jesse, I wish you all of the luck in the world up yonder," he said as the last paper was signed. "Right in the middle of God's own country."

"Thanks."

"Can I buy you lunch?" he asked, his lips twitching nervously, a little bead of sweat on his face.

"Sure."

I expected he was going to take me to lunch, but he didn't. He said to go over to Callie's Bar and Buffet across the tracks and eat on him. He handed me a blue meal ticket and walked out the doors wishing me well. I was just as happy to eat alone over at the restaurant, though, to get away from his shifty ass.

The next day, three of my cousins, Nard boys from my mama's side of the family, helped me move almost everything Mama owned, beds to refrigerator, moved it all to the house in Mount Olive. They were home from working offshore near Grand Isle.

I'd not seen Uncle Red yet, hadn't tried hard to see him, and I guess we had some words yet to say about my not staying home to take care of Mama when I was trying to manage my leave. It was a funny thing for him to hold this against me, hard and set.

On the final trip of the day, after buying everyone beer and barbeque sandwiches from the Hard-Row, I drove alone. I took with me some pictures from the walls, Mama's rent house nearly stripped, and brought Johnny, who rode in the cab with me, his body stiff on the seat, his jaw propped on my leg. He would leave the only place he had ever known except for Aunt Cat's house for the few months it took Mama to die of lung cancer. He, too, would have a new home.

At Mount Olive I walked through the door and flipped on the big box fan in the bedroom window, glad the electricity was on. I stretched out on the bed after a few minutes and heard Johnny snoring, and wondered if I would be able to sleep in Mount Olive as clear and clean as the dog did on the floor. Then the snoring sounds faded as I dozed off, drifting away into the black night air.

The next morning about daylight, Sunday, I awoke with a start, coming fast out of a deep and restful sleep. Johnny was barking in short chops down the hall. He was a good watchdog, small but alert, and I got up out of bed and walked down the center hall in my new old house, somewhat alarmed by the dog's crazy yapping.

Only wearing my white cotton drawers and a gray T-shirt with ARMY stenciled across the chest, I opened the front door. Just then, Johnny shot out the door running wide-assed open. I stepped onto the porch, the morning cool creeping across my skin making goose bumps on my forearms. I heard a growl, the sound of another dog, and I sprinted to the edge of the porch.

There before me stood a man taller and stouter than me, six-six maybe, and at least two hundred and eighty pounds. He had thick white beard hair falling around his face under a felt cowboy hat weathered way past the point of ruin.

The mountain of a man saw me. He was standing near the biggest yellow-haired pit bull I've ever seen, a dog with ears cropped, pointed ears as sharp as spikes.

The man was twenty feet away and Johnny started baying and barking at the bulldog, a stiff-haired buckskin-colored bulldog with a tar-black nose.

I saw a gun in the man's bear-paw hands, what looked like a 30-30 carbine, a Marlin from the looks of it, with the side-action ejector.

"Johnny," I hollered as the bulldog made a lunge toward the porch where I stood, Johnny between us. I ran into the yard and grabbed the beagle-mix up like a baby.

The man whistled to call the giant bulldog and he came back to him slow and made growling moans. They were the growls common among vicious dogs, but even more common among the killers of other dogs, the pit bulls. It was perhaps the sound of a feral wolf growling in front of me. All of the pit bulls I'd seen before were born and bred to rip the flesh of other dogs, of hogs in the woods, of cows, and men. This one was no different from the others, only a hell of a lot bigger.

"What business do you have here?" I asked the big man standing there with the rifle.

I shielded my chest with the dog like I was holding a gift, a sacrifice headed to the flames, looking real convincing in my cotton drawers.

"No sir, I ask the questions round here. What kind of business do you have to dwell in my place?" the man asked.

I was stunned by his question. "I bought this house from Tickfaw State Bank in Ruthberry. I bought it from the bank on Friday."

"You bought yourself nothing but trouble. I was born in that back room over yonder. I run my cows on this land. I've got an interest in it. You ought not to of come out here. You've bought yourself all kinds of trouble coming here."

His words were like mysteries. He was speaking with his teeth clenched. Right then, I thought I had no hope of getting away from his bullet, a bullet shot at point-blank range from his deer rifle.

"Sir, I own this property. I paid twenty-eight thousand dollars for it and I have a clear deed to this place. I don't know who you are or why you're in this yard."

"Name's Balem Moxley. My blood kin has owned this ground for over a hundred years. No matter if'n the bank says they own it or not. They stoled it after my little sister died. Don't matter none to me. I never handed over my birthright."

"Mr. Moxley, you need to leave." I stood there, unwilling to move.

He held the gun to his shoulder. Not aiming it, just holding the barrel toward the ground as if he was about to raise it and pull the damn trigger. "Man can't give what God a-mighty has already gived. Man can't take it away. You'll do well to find some other place before the birds pick at your flesh and the dogs howl over your bones."

The giant took his eyes off of me and Johnny. He didn't point the gun at me but still kept it to his shoulder for a few seconds, muzzle toward the ground.

He looked at me again. "You got seventy-two hours to take yourself and your dog out of here. Wednesday at this here time. Go get your money back from that bank and get the hell off my place. I said seventy-two hours."

Moxley whistled again at the pit bull, hollered, "Come Saul!" The pair walked into the thick woods out east of the house.

I watched him walk away. My gut was in twists of circled knots, my neck stinging from strain. My shoulders throbbed.

One thing was sure, and I spoke my thoughts out loud as I watched the big man go from sight: Jesse, you've gone and bought yourself a nice little problem in this good country place of yours.

CHAPTER 4

I had no phone at the house. Not yet. The phone company hadn't connected the line. A line was run to the house but there wasn't a dial tone. I didn't have a gun at the house either. Every one of my guns was stolen while I was away in the Army, a break-in at Mama's place two or three years ago.

I looked at Johnny, the dog standing at the front door wanting out, begging for a piece of the big bulldog, certain death for him and probably me too.

In the Army, I never really felt abandoned, never felt like I was left for the buzzards to circle my corpse. I felt plenty alone there and then, and I wondered for the first time in weeks why I left the Army to start with. What good did leaving the Army do? What did coming home do to change things for me in Baxter Parish?

I finally got my wits and put on some blue jeans. I loaded Johnny into the bed of the pickup truck and drove a mile to J.P. Kent's Grocery, a small convenience store with a pay phone attached to a creosote pole by the blacktop. I called the law.

While I waited, I wrote out a report of what happened in the spiral-bound notebook I kept in the truck, a report like I'd write back in Supply when something came up missing. I keep a notebook with me, a practice I started when I began my job in the Army. I didn't leave anything out, but wrote it just the way it happened.

I sat there on the tailgate. The law didn't come right away, so I bought a Coca-Cola and gassed up the truck, waited some more, Johnny sitting on the tailgate beside me as I drank from the can.

At seven o'clock sharp, a white Baxter Parish Sheriff's Office cruiser pulled into the gravel parking lot. The deputy was probably my age, with his narrow face and blond hair. The little rectangle nameplate on his chest said DEP. K. McLin.

I remarked right off that I was soon to become a deputy sheriff myself, Monday morning. Then I settled into the story about what happened, and how the man doing the threatening was named Balem Moxley, and how I didn't know him from Adam's housecat.

Deputy Kurt McLin corrected me shaking his head. "That's Cotton Moxley. Nobody calls him Balem."

"What do you intend to do about him coming into my yard with a rifle and telling me to leave the place by Wednesday morning?"

He studied the ground for a second, swiping his foot across the gravel and dirt. "Well, nothing. Do you have the place legally posted with four foot of hog wire and two strands of barbed wire, No Trespassing signs up and down the fence line?"

"No."

"Good buddy, we can't do a thing. It's a civil matter," he said. "Unless he does something to your person, we can't do a thing." He looked away from me when he spoke, staring out across the horizon, as if he was reading from a great scroll somewhere off in the distance, or perhaps he simply didn't want to make eye contact.

"Well," he added, "if Cotton comes back on your place, call us and we'll run him off. I need to tell you this, Tadlock, off the record." He leaned into me, eyeballing me for the first time. "Cotton Moxley is not to be toyed with. Stay the hell away from him. Don't forget what I'm telling you. Stay the hell away from that man."

The deputy turned around with his last word and went back to his car and drove off. He didn't even make a report, and I could tell that his leaving was complete and total. I figured it wasn't much point calling him again.

But the whole business made no sense. The deputy didn't do a damned thing. He didn't do shit. So I went back to the phone and looked up the number to the sheriff, his home number listed in the white pages of the Baxter Parish directory. I got on the phone and called Haltom Roberts. However, all I got was an answering machine, and I relayed what happened that morning, a long message that lasted till the recorder quit and I got a dial tone.

I went back to the truck and shut the tailgate. Johnny had his head resting on the bedrail. Anger welled up inside my chest and around me, and I wanted something done about that son of a bitch coming into my yard the way he did.

It wasn't yet eight o'clock when I arrived back at the house. I went on and took a hot shower, put on some dress clothes, a pressed striped shirt and a pair of khaki pants. I wiped off my black leather dress shoes.

There was but one thing to do: go to church. That's the way it was growing up. If times got tough, and they did often, we'd pack up and go to church, Sunday morning or Wednesday night, down in Packwood Corners at the Fundamental Gospel Church. We'd go back like we'd never missed a service. If somebody died, or something bad came sailing down the pike, something too damn big for us to handle, we'd go to the church house. Somebody might criticize, say we were superstitious. Who cares? Maybe Mama and me were just a little bit Christ-haunted was all.

"No matter where you've gone or how you've fallen away, get right up and dust yourself plumb off and get back to God the next Sunday," Mama would say. "You'll find God right where you left him," she said many times during my life. That's what I thought I ought to do.

I didn't attend church regularly while in the Army, not unless there was a problem. Sometimes I did have a problem; maybe trouble with an officer or homesickness, or the general gloom of being in the service. I'd make chapel, try to get my bearings straight. It seemed to do me good.

There was a little church I'd seen a few miles away from the house. The church was on Highway 38, Ridgecrest Baptist Church.

I was going to church because of Moxley's threats. If that's selfish or superstitious, I'm guilty of both. I planned to go to church and dwell on the evil of the day, and perhaps find some flashing glimpse of hope that might await me, some answers to part the silence. I was hoping for some peace, if it could be had. So be it on June 11, 1989, I thought. By God I'll go on to church.

I left the house at ten-thirty, and the whole ride over to Ridgecrest Church, I couldn't get my head unwrapped from around the image of Moxley's face in my yard. The second image was of the piece-of-crap deputy, and I made a mental note to stay away from him when I started work for the Sheriff's Office.

What should I think about the incident? I realized that Moxley's coming over might have gotten it off his chest, the way a bully's threats can be enough to satisfy him sometimes. I wondered if it was just empty threats.

I slowed to pull into the church parking lot. The steel building resembled a large mechanic's garage, a white steeple on top showed the dull shine of aluminum, a flashing pointer sign out front of the church carried a message in plastic letters: "THERE'S NO STOP, DROP, AND ROLL IN HELL." Maybe thirty cars and pickups lined the gravel lot. I figured I might be able to slip in near the back and remain unnoticed. I needed to pray and sing, just do what I knew to do when something wasn't going right.

The preacher stood at the door of the church greeting people. Sunday school must have just let out; children frolicked in their best clothes, pretty skirts flowing around little girls' knees. I shook the pastor's hand and he asked my name. He introduced me to a couple of men standing by the back pew, not one wearing a tie.

I wanted some peace, but shortly after I sat down with my King James Bible in my lap, a slim woman in a green dress with sparkling fingernails like talons gripped a microphone on the stage and began to sing a solo as the piano played. She sang a chorus three times through: "Power, power, power to do God's will…Power, power, power to know God's ways…Power, power, power to know God's name, all the power that the Lord Jesus brings." She was testing the microphone and it grated when she started shouting, "testing, testing, testing, one, two, three, four, testing." Then a man walked up to the stage and adjusted a piece of electronic equipment, and the speakers squealed, making an awful popping sound.

I was sitting there watching all of this activity. Then something like I'd never seen before in my entire life moved into full view on the stage. I did a double take and realized that it was an itty bitty human man perched on a skateboard, dressed in a dark suit. It looked like a midget wearing a red paisley tie. I saw tiny shoes and what looked like stubby legs poking out about a foot in front of the skateboard. Then the slim gospel singer walked over and squatted down and kissed the midget before my very eyes.

Somebody handed me a program, a gray photocopied thing that made me want to leave right off. The headline on the church bulletin said, "End-Time Evangelist Calloway Holland, World's Shortest Preacher." I read that the man was born deformed, that he was only twenty-nine inches tall, and that he used a skateboard to move around. He was there to preach a revival and this was the first service. The woman singing the song was his own wife, Glorietta Jane.

Before I could get out of the pew and haul ass, a family glared at me, glares from child to the mother. Then they asked me to move down. One of the kids said I was "in their pew." I'd forgotten how Southern Baptists sometimes claim their pews and aren't beyond fist fighting over the place they sit on Sunday mornings. I moved down, a mistake indeed. The service got started right away, and I was wedged in between people I didn't know. The pew was narrow, impossible to scoot through to the end of the aisle without causing a stir. I was in quite a jam and knew it.

The preacher whose hand I'd shaken earlier got up and read the announcements, introduced Brother Holland, and said that we were in for a "real good gospel treat." The stunted midget evangelist rolled across the unadorned wooden stage, and I swear, as God is my witness, he popped a wheelie with the skateboard and waved to the crowd.

The singing commenced again, old hymns with piano playing, the notes banged hard. An ancient man stood at the cedar wood pulpit and led the music with his arms swinging at his chest to keep the people in time with the song. We sang "Victory in Jesus" and "Jesus Paid It All" and "There Is a Fountain Filled with Blood." We sang some of the choruses twice through for added fervor and emphasis: "There is a fountain filled with blood drawn from Emmanuel's veins; and sinners plunged beneath that flood lose all their guilty stains."

The singing slowed and the evangelist's bespectacled wife sang a song I'd never heard before: "The end time is coming, the end time is coming, oh the Lord God will reap with vengeance, all the seeds that you have sown," one line went.

Then everything died down, and the crippled evangelist rolled up to the edge of the stage like he was about to slide right off and break his fool neck. He read from a worn black leather Bible, and I winced at his choice of scripture.

He garbled his words a little as he read into the microphone. I could have understood it with no problem but for the people murmuring in the pews all around me. He chose a passage from the end of the Book of Revelation, and he said that this would be the Sunday of judgment for Ridgecrest Church. He said that he was going to bring us a sword, not a plowshare.

The preacher's voice was as malformed as his body. It sounded like Daffy Duck and Tweety Bird with a case of palsy. There was a slight delay between what I heard him say and when I understood it. He shouted, "Jesus is coming soon. Are you ready? Are-you-ready? Oh, no, you're like that Great Harlot in Revelations the seventeenth chapter of God's Holy Bible."

Some old man with cauliflower ears sat in front of me. He must have been hard of hearing. "Delah," he asked his old wife, "is that little preacher a pigmy? I have many times wanted to see a live pigmy." He asked plenty loud enough for people to hear three pews back and forth.

The woman swatted him with her hand. "No, he's just a little midget preacher. Be quiet," she said.

I squirmed in my seat. I wished I'd driven to Packwood Corners for church.

The little evangelist read from the book. "And I saw the woman drunken with the blood of the saints." His mouth began to froth with a line of saliva. "And with the blood of the martyrs of Jesus: and when I saw her, I wondered with great admiration." Then he turned the book to the nineteenth chapter. "For true and righteous are his judgments: for he hath judged the great whore, which did corrupt the earth with her fornication, and hath avenged the blood of his servants at her hand."

I could feel the tension rise in the room as if someone had just lit a gasoline fire in front of us.

"You're whores," he screamed. "You're like brazen harlots." The preacher rolled back across the barren stage, pointing his gnarled finger, doing his best to keep from falling off into the wooden steps. He had a wire harness around his neck to keep the microphone attached to him as he skated, the Bible in his lap, and his hands moved him along the stage similar to the way an ape trots across a jungle floor.

He stopped all of a sudden and read more verses: "The beast was taken, and with him the false prophet that wrought miracles before him, with which he deceived them that had received the mark of the beast, and them that worshipped his image. These both were cast alive into a lake of fire burning with brimstone.

"The Bible says you'll be cast into the depths of a burning hell. You've left your first love and claim with Christ for ways of idolatry. You've accepted the mark of the beast. You're like gyps in heat begging for the next stud dog to come along and give you service. You don't tithe your income, you don't support the work of the ministry, and all you care about is yourselves and your own money. All you care about is dairy cows and new tractors. Whores, the Bible calls you whores!" The evangelist kept on, goading and insulting, quoting scriptures from memory, slurring his words, dripping spit down his chin.

There were no amens for the little man in the three-piece suit; nevertheless, all eyes were pointed at his every move.

The preaching went on for near an hour. It started bad and got worse. He told stories about how he used to sleep with prostitutes, how he did drugs for years and years, every kind of dope from weed to heroin. He said he was overcome with a demonic foot fetish for Oriental women. He'd gone totally astray till he met the Lord Jesus face to face in a mission church on Bourbon Street in New Orleans. During the preaching, he spun circles on his skateboard, two wheels in the air. I thought he was going to fall off the stage any second.

I admit that I was taken by the little preacher. I was disgusted, but taken. For a while my mind was off my troubles at home, but like all things, the service finally had to end, the first service of five days straight, according to the paper bulletin. During the altar call at the close of the preaching, no one walked forward to be cleansed of their sins. The church people sat as stones while the music leader motioned to the beat of the gospel hymn, "Have thine own way, Lord! Have thine own way! Thou art the Potter; I am the clay. Mold me and make me after thy will, while I am waiting, yielded and still."

When the hymn played out, there was a long-winded prayer by a gray-headed man sitting up toward the front of the church on the left side, a prayer asking Jesus to send the preacher off to where he could be used even more fully than at Ridgecrest, as if he'd forgotten this was a five-day revival.

The people filed out the door like the place was on fire. It was a mad rush for the door. No one walked up to the evangelist, who stayed on the stage to shake hands. It appeared that the church folks wanted no part of the little preacher or his wife, who knelt beside him, wiping spit from his chin with a silk handkerchief.

The old man in the pew in front of me stood. He spoke to another old codger that had the swollen hands of a dairyman. "Roderick, I believe that was the craziest thing I seen in my whole life since Leonard Jerry got naked with a she-goat."

The dairyman frowned. "Brother Kendall has him some explaining to do come deacons' meeting. I suspect he might'n be the she-goat if he ain't careful on Wednesday night."

I knew all hell was about to break loose for Brother Kendall, and I can't say he didn't need firing. I was about to leave, walk right by the pastor, join the people rushing out the door, when I began to hear the crying of women, one high pitched, the other low. There was a line to the door and people were trying to move fast down the center aisle. They were overtaking me. Folks were pushing and shoving one another, almost running in fright, looking back at the deformed midget evangelist on the stage. No one stopped to speak to me or offer the least welcome.

The crying noise turned my head around and I saw a lady at the end of a pew on the floor. She was nearly trampled by the congregation, a woman I hadn't seen earlier in the service, a woman with hair as dark as a Puerto Rican's, shiny hair that appeared as onyx from twenty feet away. The woman was making the sobbing noise, I could tell, and a child perhaps eight years old stood in the aisle beside the pew crying.

I stopped. Almost everyone was out of the church except for that crazy-assed midget preacher and his wife. A wrinkled woman walked by me scowling, and I watched as the young girl began to pull at the lady's arm, but she wouldn't stop. People left the building as if God himself couldn't stop them.

I was a stranger in a strange place at Ridgecrest Baptist Church. I wasn't from the north end of the parish. I knew no one at this house of worship. In the Army, the church was all-military, and that was a kind of bond. I was there this Sunday for comfort, to comfort myself from my mama's death and my own misfortune in Mount Olive. Standing in the church sanctuary, I realized for the first time that I was out of place in the north end of the parish.

I found myself standing over the fallen woman. She was wearing a skirt made of thick cotton. "Ma'am, are you all right?"

She didn't respond at first. She was clutching her ankle. Her shoulders were shaking.

"I can't get up. I've done twisted my ankle." She looked at me.

Tears were rolling down her sharp-bone cheeks.

The little girl reached down to her mama and tried to lift her, as if she might move her by some kind of magic strength. Then the girl cried all the more, dancing around in the aisle like an ant spinning in a pool of oil. "Please help my mommy," she said, "please help, please." The child jigged to some unheard music tingling her ears. I noticed green bruises up and down her skinny arms.

"Baby, it's going to be all right. I'll take care of it," I told her.

I squatted beside the woman and hoisted her by the armpits, letting her get a good grasp of me as I pulled her up and helped her sit in the pew.

"Can you walk?"

"No."

"You think it's broken?"

"Feels as such."

"Ma'am, I'll get some help," I said.

I found the pastor outside. He was waving his hand at a passing car from the church doorway. He followed me back inside the building.

The evangelist was still on the stage, watching us like we were in some sort of freak show. His wife continued wiping the drool from his suit coat with the handkerchief. The entire congregation was gone.

The pastor called the woman Nokomis; he surveyed her like she was a coon with its paw stuck in a steel trap. "What in the world did you do?" the preacher said.

"Got up," she said. "That's all I done. When the service ended, Brother Kendall, I just got up and my ankle gived out."

"Uhm," he said. "I hope you don't think we're going to pay for a trip to the hospital." There was an indignant tone in his voice and I immediately hated the man. I wanted to choke him right there in the house of God.

"Where's your ride?" he asked.

"We got dropped off by my husband. He told us to walk home but I can't walk them miles hurt like this here," the woman said.

"I got to go to McComb City to take the evangelist to eat at the Dinner Bell. I can't carry y'all home. Car'll be full with our wives." He crunched his shoulders, shrugged.

It was the damndest thing. The preacher went and got the evangelist and the gospel singer and made a beeline for the door and left.

"Ma'am, you need a ride? Can I take you to a doctor?"

"A ride, but no doctors. We just live a little piece away."

I helped the woman outside, letting her hang onto my shoulder to walk. There weren't any cars visible anywhere in the lot.

I loaded them into the truck. It was me and the girl and the woman in the cab of my pickup, and an odd thing happened as we drove away. The woman wasn't much older than me, mid-thirties I'd guess, though her skin was almost tanned leather from work in the fields or hay pastures maybe. I observed that her face quit grimacing when she got into the truck. Directly, as we entered the highway, she put her arm over the back of the seat behind the girl and began fingering my neck. It shocked the hell out of me.

On Highway 38 I watched a possum lurch across the road and back into the ditch up ahead, then straight into my tire, plop, then I watched it as dead meat on the road through my rearview mirror. I was trying to see this woman's arm at my neck. The girl didn't say two words the whole ride, sitting between us sucking her left thumb. Our Bibles, three of them, were spread across the dashboard.

Once we got on Spears Road, the woman said, "Turn here. The road'll tear your truck to pieces if you ain't one to drive slow."

After a few minutes easing down the rutted logging path well behind my place, back in the woods perhaps a half mile, we came to a clearing. Good God, I thought. I saw the ridge of a rusted tin roof, and dogs stretched for acres, and chickens in little teepee huts made of dented tin. It all came alive, barking and cackling like daybreak. The dogs had great skulls as thick as hyenas, all sizes and shapes and colors. Some dogs had houses, some had oil drums, and others had nothing but bare chains around their necks.

I saw cages with raccoons near a barn, live foxes, and what looked like skunks, all in raised wire cages. I even saw a big steel cage that looked like it held a pair of coyotes.

The roosters near the house were tied by the drumstick with cords, and their bodies crouched as silhouettes on sticks above the ground underneath their A-frame huts.

The noise of frothing dogs and crowing chickens almost caused me to stop the pickup cold. Instead, I slid to a slow grind, my ears ringing in my head. Nokomis still rubbed on my neck. I should have asked her to quit touching me, but I was so surprised by it that I didn't know what to do. We stopped in front of the house.

I opened the truck door and stepped into the grassless yard. Before me stood a weathered house covered in black tarpaper and rotten boards with a sagging porch across the front; it was surrounded by sweet gum trees.

I let them out of the truck and the woman thanked me for helping. I was watching for a biting dog. I offered to help her inside, but she declined.

"If you ever need a thing, I'm Nokomis Moxley. I'll do what I can for you, baby."

Just as I was about to say good-bye, her name shot straight through my heart like a hot piece of steel, and I saw the giant man walk out on the porch with his head kind of bent down at a slight angle and I realized who it was and where in the hell I had arrived.

I shut my truck door and backed out watching the girl and her mama hobble to the steps, gripping each other for support. Above them stood the big monster of a man on the porch, looming.

CHAPTER 5

When I arrived at my house after the church service, I loaded up Johnny in the cab of the pickup for the half-hour drive down I-55 to Pickleyville and over to Packwood Corners. I was going to eat lunch with Uncle Red and Aunt Latrice, together with them both for the first time since I got back to Packwood Corners. In addition to this, I had arranged a late-afternoon date with Penny.

I knew Aunt Latrice was trying to smooth things over between Uncle Red and me, and I needed some allies fast, but I didn't relish the visit. I thought long and hard while I drove, wishing I could ditch the lunch. Knowing my survival in Mount Olive probably meant having ample backup, I went on to their house.

I was planning to call the sheriff again and maybe even the chief deputy, and I aimed to get any gun that Uncle Red would loan me.

The first thing I did when I got to Uncle Red's was to grab an old rusted cane knife and a slat of oak carved smooth and round like a club out of his truck. The oak was something he used to beat catfish unconscious while fishing, blood stains on one end of it. I would ask his permission later. I wanted more help as I packed these back to my own pickup and stowed them away in case I needed them later.

Aunt Latrice had a pork roast warming in a brown crock pot, and the smell of garlic and onions and cooked meat went into my nose and eyes and lungs the second I stepped through the screen door. Aunt Cat was at the table smoking unfiltered Pall Malls, wearing her signature red lipstick. I hugged both her and Aunt Latrice, but no one kissed me. We hug women in my family but don't kiss them. To kiss another man's wife, even on the cheek, where I come from is to invite yourself into a feud.

Johnny scratched at the screen door. I told him to stop. He stood there like a brown haze at the bottom of the mesh wire screen. I hollered at him again and he sloughed away from the door.

I could see Uncle Red napping in the living room, stretched out on a stuffed recliner, a political show wafting sounds into the kitchen. His silhouette, broad nose at the peak of his outline, reminded me of every Sunday in my childhood.

Aunt Latrice handed me a glass of iced tea without asking if I cared for one. I hadn't seen Uncle Red since returning home and I was uneasy. Just hadn't seen him. I wasn't sure what to think or do after what he said on the phone months ago, the way he acted at the funeral.

No question, I needed some partners in this war where the first shots were already being fired. Uncle Red wasn't to be toyed with, and this could go for or against my favor.

My uncle walked into the kitchen after a few minutes, but he didn't say anything. Just walked past me on the other side of the table and grabbed the newspaper from the countertop by the toaster oven. He walked big and cumbersome, and didn't speak to anyone. As he went back through the living room archway, he turned around and gazed at me for the first time. "Son, how's that place of yours up yonder? I've been too busy, but meaning to come up there and take a look at it myself. Been real busy with nets and slat traps, fishing a lot."

"I got trouble," I admitted. I was almost ashamed to tell them, worried about how they might receive my walking into a hornet's nest in Mount Olive.

He raised one eyebrow. "What kind of trouble?"

I told them all about moving in the day before without a snag, and how at the break of light that morning some damned enormous bastard came up out of the woods and said for me to leave and gave me seventy-two hours to do it.

Aunt Cat's eyes bugged when I spoke. She took a new cigarette down to the ash in three draws, smoke billowing out of her nose and mouth, and she crushed it in an ashtray that looked like a miniature car tire with Firestone embossed on one side in white letters.

"Goddamn, son, you say you called Haltom Roberts at home?" Uncle Red asked.

"Yes sir. No answer, a machine, an answering machine took my message."

Uncle Red had the look of disdain on his face towering over the table, a rolled up newspaper still in his hand like a ball bat. His forehead wore tight wrinkles, horizontal lines from worry and sun. I could see how he'd aged, now fifty-seven years old. "I'll call him," he said.

He did call right away, but he was faced with the same telephone answering machine. It was as useless to him as it was to me. "You say a deputy warned you?" Uncle Red asked after he hung up the phone on the wall.

I nodded. "The man's name is Balem Moxley. The deputy who came out was a McLin, and he told me that Moxley goes by "Cotton." The deputy warned me to stay away from Moxley in no uncertain terms. Moxley seems to be the resident badass of north Baxter. The worst of it was that I ended up taking Moxley's old lady and girl home. His wife fell and twisted her ankle at church up in Mount Olive this morning. I didn't know who she was till I drove up in the yard and saw her old man there as big as sin. Nobody at the church would help her; she'd been originally planning to walk two or three miles home."

"Son of a bitch," he said. My uncle scratched his head. "Balem Moxley? From Mount Olive, you say?"

"A neighbor. Brother to the woman who owned the place before she killed herself."

He scratched his scalp some more. "I believe I might know a Moxley."

"Yes."

"I believe he's one of those crazy-assed-up shitheads that used to work turn-arounds in the plants. They were all big and bad to steal. Yeah, them Moxleys were electricians. I think I know who you're talking about, the family."

We sat down and ate. The conversation never strayed far from Moxley and the deputy sheriff.

When we were done with the meal, Uncle Red told me to come outside with him and we talked out in the yard, the sun warm but not unbearable under the shade trees. He asked me if I had a gun, and I said I didn't and that I aimed to borrow one if he was willing to lend. We talked about my strategy to handle the problems up in Mount Olive and I confessed that I didn't have any real strategy. Not yet. He wanted me to change the locks on the doors right away.

We went back inside and the women were in the living room watching TV. Uncle Red brought me into his and Aunt Latrice's bedroom. He pulled out from the closet a Winchester .22 magnum lever-action rifle with a telescopic sight. I had seen the rifle before, had watched Uncle Red use it to shoot a mink once back at his chicken house. Uncle Red gave me a box of fifty shells for the .22 magnum. Then he went to the dresser drawer and retrieved a revolver wrapped in a red and white cloth. It was a .38 police special, stainless steel, and he fished out a box of bullets for it and also a leather holster that fit it tight. He told me to load both of them and I did. Nine shells in the rifle, six in the revolver. We walked out the sliding glass door from the bedroom out onto a patio porch. We took the guns to my pickup in the yard silent, not letting the women see or hear us.

"You don't aim for that sumbitch to run you off, do you?"

"I aim for him not to. Hell, I'm a deputy sheriff as of eight o'clock in the morning."

"We'll both go visit that big cotton-headed bastard with a length of pipe if we need to." He smiled, trying to reassure me.

"I know. Hey, I borrowed your machete and fish club. I got them before I came inside earlier."

"No problem," he said.

We went back into the kitchen and I left with a plate of food covered in aluminum foil. I had to put Johnny in the bed of the truck to keep him from getting into the food and he looked like he enjoyed the wind and the warm sunlight and the chance to see the world from back there, his head hanging over the side. He barked occasionally, not seeing anything, just barking in joy, the pleasure of riding in the wind and barking like a dog.

Behind the seat lay the rifle and scope, the pistol beside me. In the glove box was the silver flashlight that Uncle Red gave me, right next to my old set of handcuffs. The cane knife and wooden club were on the floorboard. I watched Johnny in the rearview mirror off and on all the way back to Pickleyville, hoping he'd behave himself and not get carried away barking and jumping around the truck bed and fall into the concrete interstate highway while I drove to see Penny.

CHAPTER 6

I told Penny I would stop by her house on Piney Woods Street in Pickleyville, over near the Mormon church. I was in no real shape for a date, and I knew I needed to go on up to Mount Olive and change the locks, see what other mischief was afoot.

I was supposed to be at her house at two o'clock. We were going to see a movie and eat dinner at Jack Mel's Restaurant downtown, a converted old mansion with white tablecloths and roast duck, but I had Johnny and needed to take care of business.

As promised, I found her place with little trouble. It was a cypress shotgun house under a canopy of drooping oaks. A garden of vines and willow trees surrounded the cottage, which was painted in pastels of yellows and blues.

I knocked on the door at the little stoop, a door with a glass transom above it.

Penny opened the door and smiled, beaming. She kissed me on the neck, invited me inside.

"How are you, Jesse?" she said.

I hesitated. "I wish better, not so good." We sat in the little living room on stuffed chairs. I told her what happened in Mount Olive, the story from beginning to end, from Moxley and the bulldog to the church service to the deputy sheriff's coldness.

"My God. What do you plan to do?" she asked.

"I'm not sure I know, but Uncle Red gave me some guns and told me to change the locks. I'm kind of in a fog. Only in Baxter Parish can buying a simple piece of land lead to all this trouble. It's just the craziest place on earth."

"My father used to say the parish was paved in trouble."

"Yeah. That's right. Penny, I was wondering under the circumstances if I could give you a raincheck on our dinner." I felt really bad saying this.

"Sure, but be careful. Don't make yourself a stranger."

"I appreciate it and I won't be a stranger if you don't want me to be."

Johnny barked outside in the back of the pickup, two short yaps.

"Was that your dog?"

"Yeah, he's in my truck, Mama's beagle."

"Is he your dog now?"

"I guess so. I figure I ought to keep him."

"That's good of you. I wouldn't think much of person who didn't."

"I'll take care of him till he dies."

She kind of looked down at her feet for a bit, then looked back into my face. "If I can do something, just let me know."

We both stood to go out the door.

"I mean it," she said. "Call me."

"OK, Penny. Will do. Maybe we can get together Tuesday. I start work tomorrow with the Sheriff's Office."

"I bet the guy in Mount Olive won't like that."

"Probably not."

"Good, let's make it Tuesday night."

"I'll call tomorrow evening when I get a work schedule, my hours."

We said our good-byes and I drove to Kmart and bought new locks for the exterior doors, a set of two so that I had one key to fit both doors. Johnny was there in the back of the truck the whole time as happy as a water-drenched hog. Then I got back on I-55 and headed to the house.

CHAPTER 7

When I got to the house that afternoon, I changed the locks. This took two hours. Afterward, I started unpacking everything, cleaning with a wet rag, trying to straighten up the house. I mopped all the floors, then the shelves and cabinets with Parson's ammonia and water, the smell strong but worth it, all of the windows and doors open for ventilation, the screen doors shut to ward off Johnny.

When I bought the house it had been emptied and left free of any furniture or trash, but it wasn't really clean. It was dusty and musty and full of mold. A moldy film spread across everything there like an organic skin of some kind.

After the floor was dry, Johnny would walk in and out of the house; he was quiet, not barking or whining. The dog was alert but not real yappy, and that was good. If he barked, I would know to go get the pistol or the rifle from the bedroom. I heard the sound of a log truck on the highway a half mile up the road, and it made me jump as I cleaned the wooden cabinet under the porcelain sink, and I nearly busted my head open beneath the wooden counter, jumping at the sound of the slightest noise.

I spent four hours unpacking and cleaning, sorting things to throw away. I later sat on the screen porch out back and drank a cold beer from the refrigerator. It was getting dark out and fatigue was wearing on me heavy.

My bare foot ran across Johnny's coarse belly, and I drained the beer looking out into the night. The pistol sat on the round cedar table I brought from Mama's place. I had a pair of pressed black pants and my Army-issue dress shoes polished to a mirror-shine, and a white oxford cloth shirt with a button-down collar hung beside the trousers in Mama's upright cedar chest in the bedroom. I was ready for the first day of work.

My mind wandered as I sat. I thought of Penny and wished she were with me while I worked in the house.

I carried the pistol while walking out to the lean-to carport, and I loaded Johnny into the front of the truck, and we drove into the night, down the country roads. One of the worst parts of Army life was the lack of freedom to do this, to gather your thoughts at the drop of a hat, to drive the gravel roads and narrow two-lane blacktops and see what was out in the country. Johnny slept on the seat near the gun, right where a woman might sit if I had one with me at the time, not all the way over to the passenger side, but sitting kind of close to me.

It was eight-thirty and I drove over to the store and called the sheriff again, thinking I might find Roberts at home. I told the damned machine that I had trouble, and I would try to see him Monday morning when I went to work, that I didn't have a phone yet but I would indeed see him. Of course, I got nothing better than the click when the recording was over, no real person on the other end of the line.

To my surprise the convenience store was still open. I went inside the little grocery, leaving Johnny in the cab of the truck with the windows cranked down. I bought myself a Budweiser and made small talk with the shriveled-up old man behind the counter. He was thin with the stature of someone near ruin, frail and ashy-skinned.

"You ever heard of Balem Moxley?" I asked, trying to slip it into conversation, having already talked about fishing the Tangilena River a moment earlier.

The man hushed. He eyed me like he was trying to read my thoughts. "Cotton," he corrected. "Folks call him Cotton." He craned his face toward the glass door across the counter, as if to see if anybody was coming.

"Son, he stole me blind. I was a dairyman up here before I bought this store. I also ran hogs in the river swamp, a hundred marked sows, back in the mid-sixties and early seventies. One by one that asshole poached my pigs. He'd trap them or take them with them damned bulldogs of his. If he couldn't catch one to steal and sell, he'd kill it in the woods, shoot it and leave it to rot for the vultures.

"In 1974 we went to trial over the fact he sold some of my marked hogs at the auction in Franklinton and a buddy of mine seen it. I be damned if Sheriff Roberts ain't showed up in the open court and testified that he seen Cotton buy them hogs at the Thursday Ruthberry livestock sale the month before, bought for cash money outside at a trailer instead of in the ring the way you're supposed to buy stock. Cotton had no papers whatsoever to show that he bought them. Paid cash. No name of the feller what he bought them from. Goddamned lying under oath, what it was. Oh, but he had the sheriff's word on it, and that's as good as the stamp of Mr. All-Mighty Jesus hisself around here."

"What's your name?" he asked.

"Jesse Tadlock."

"Well, Tadlock, Cotton declared when he left the parish courthouse down in Ruthberry—he was acquitted, mind you—that he wouldn't sleep nary a wink till he stole every hog I had in the woods and sold or killed every damned cow. Him laughing when he told it out on the courthouse lawn; a half-dozen witnesses heard it.

"By God he done just that. Poisoned the last of my heifers with lime in the fields. Forty Holsteins dead in two weeks. I had to start this grocery for a way to eat, my wife and me. That's Cotton Moxley and you stay the hell away from him."

By this time the old man was shaking and in a fury and I was scared he might lie down and die of a heart attack in front of my eyes. I thanked him for the beer I bought and left through the glass doors.

I was afraid now of connections between Moxley and my future boss. From the looks of the old man when I left, there was plenty to fret about.

CHAPTER 8

Come Monday morning I was tired and felt almost hungover from the lack of sleep and distress the night before. It was an awful night, tossing in bed till maybe three o'clock in the morning, when I finally fell asleep. The locusts had called their tune and the sounds of crickets pelted the night air. The alarm clock's red light found me already wide awake; 6:05, the clock said, so I eased out of bed, pistol removed from the nightstand, and let Johnny out.

The pistol was cold in my hand. I slept under a thin blanket with a ceiling fan stirring the mildewy smell of the bedroom, the big box fan in the window pulling moisture into the room from outside.

I stood on the front porch. The bank's maintenance people had mowed the yard about a week earlier, according to Bullfinch. The grass was short and azalea bushes outlined the yard near the house. Johnny walked a few feet from the porch steps and lifted his leg on a dying shrub, and I took a leak off the porch myself, a stream of yellow urine sailing into the grass, the revolver hanging from my left hand.

The morning sun was beginning to break and all was calm. I hadn't seen hide nor hair of Moxley in twenty-four hours, and I hoped I'd never lay eyes on him again. If he did come back, I figured my deputy's badge would scare him off. I wasn't backing down yet, but I was concerned with what might happen. All those years my mama rented from slumlords, and then more than a decade renting stable and fair from Uncle Red, and then paying the premiums on a life insurance policy, never owning anything. I sure as hell didn't want to lay down for Moxley to walk all over me.

Back inside, I put on a pot of coffee, Community Coffee, dark roast, the best coffee I'd ever tasted. The aluminum pot on the stove was probably older than I was. I drank down two cups black and ate a bowl of oatmeal with honey and sweet milk. I later dressed in slacks and a white shirt.

When I left for the first day on the new job, I put Johnny outside. I was a little concerned, this being a new place and all, but I figured he wouldn't wander off. I positioned the .22 magnum carbine behind the Chevy truck seat and put the pistol under a red handkerchief beside me. I drove off into the morning sunlight glad to be headed to my job, a new line of work for a man returning home.

I drove down Old Highway 51 rather than the interstate, on through Kemp Station, Tangilena, Roseville, and into Ruthberry. Shanties lined the road by the railroad tracks on the eastside of the highway, not one dwelled in by white folks. I suppose things had been like this for a hundred years, the social order almost a caste system of haves and have-nots. I knew this bit of history, and it didn't make me too happy.

Once in Ruthberry, I parked the truck under a pin oak tree in the shade, so as to keep the pickup cool during the day. The courthouse was around the corner and the Sheriff's Office was quiet, too early yet for employees. It was seven-thirty, and I decided to go buy a newspaper. I did, grabbing a copy of the *Ruthberry Ledger* from a white box under the courthouse porch, paying my quarter.

The front-page stories were filled with blood, a carload of people run over by a train in Milltown, all dead; an acetylene gas explosion at the junior college where a construction company was building a new dorm, one man blown through the air sixty feet, dead as a sack full of ground beef, and another man blown into three separate pieces from the blast as well, one third of his corpse stuck in the limbs of a privet hedge. There was a shooting in Washington Park related to crack cocaine, which had invaded even rural places like a sickness, an incurable and infectious disease. The paper said the dead boy was sixteen and was shot in the skull, duct tape on his mouth.

At eight o'clock sharp, I put the newspaper on the truck seat, atop the handkerchief and pistol, atop my notebook, and locked the truck doors, stepping over to the Sheriff's Office. My white shirt was starched, my creases like knives.

I walked past the greeter woman at a wooden desk out front, and down the hall to Felix Dufrene's office. His door was locked, so I sat in a folding chair out in the hallway.

After a half hour, I went to the receptionist and asked her when Dufrene would be arriving for work.

"Mr. Dufrene is in a meeting with Sheriff Roberts. He'll be available at eight-forty-five," she said while reaching to answer a buzzing phone.

I went back down the hall and waited another thirty minutes.

Dufrene walked straight past me without speaking, a file folder in his hand. I rose as he opened his door.

"Come on in," he said without looking at me, without shaking my hand, without ever making eye contact, as if I wasn't someone he cared to see.

I sat down in front of his desk and felt tension envelop my neck, the same kind of tension I felt the day I was told Mama was dying of lung cancer.

"I'm mighty sorry Tadlock, but there was a mistake with the budget. You don't have a job with the Sheriff's Office, and you won't have a job during the '89-'90 fiscal year." After saying this he lit a cigarette with a flash of light, crushing its end after one drag.

I was stung. It was like he'd hit me in the mouth with a pair of brass knuckles. I just sat there staring at him for the longest time, unsure what to say in response.

"You might try the Ruthberry P.D. or Pickleyville or even down in Milltown if you want to work law enforcement. A number of guys got hired at the Ruthberry Foundry, they tell me, and there are some jobs at Tidwell's Grocery Warehouse near the Pickleyville airport. They might have something, but we don't," he said.

I got up without speaking, turned, and walked back to the receptionist down the hall. "My name's Jesse Tadlock and I want to speak to Sheriff Roberts. I'm a family friend. He'll see me," I said to the woman.

She called his secretary right away, said I was there to see the sheriff. The receptionist hung up the phone kind of abruptly. "The sheriff is in the field. He won't be back again today. You can call tomorrow and check if he'll see you. Call first." She picked up the phone and dialed, turning her head away from me, cupping her hand around her mouth and the phone receiver to conceal her voice.

I walked out the glass door and into the blazing sun.

Back at the truck, a note was slipped under the windshield wiper on the driver's side and at first I thought I'd gotten a damned parking ticket. I opened the note. It was handwritten on steno paper in big block letters. I read it out loud: "YOU GOT 45 HOURS TO GET THE HELL OFF THE PLACE. THE GODDAMNED CLOCK IS TICKING TADLOCK."

I stared at the note a minute, reread it. I'd had a bellyful of this bullshit and walked straight back into the Sheriff's Office, on beyond the receptionist, on past a sign pointing to Haltom Roberts's office, and through the wooden door.

His secretary asked how she could help me, and I heard Roberts's voice behind her, behind an open door, talking on the phone, it sounded like. I walked beyond her desk with the note in my hand and she followed me into his office.

The sheriff looked surprised to see me. He told whoever was on the phone that he'd call later. He motioned for me to sit down.

"Julie Lynn, it's all OK. I'll talk to Jesse for a few minutes. Pull the door to," he said to the long-legged woman who'd followed me into the office.

I could barely see straight. "Mr. Haltom, tell me about why all of a sudden I don't have a job? And why a son of a bitch like Balem Moxley has something to do with it?" I handed him the note across the desk. "And tell me why your deputies never respond to this shit?"

"This is just a note. What difference does it make?"

"I'd say an awful lot of difference, the difference between a job and no job."

He scanned the letter. "Jesse, boy, there's two Baxter Parishes. One starts at Lake Tickfaw and ends at Nesom, the other begins just south of Liberty City and goes to the Mississippi line. Each has its own way of doing things. You're from the south end and understand it down there. But up at the north end everything's different. I just happen to be the law for two parts of the country. I've learned how to negotiate the differences."

"What about the job?" I asked, unimpressed with his civics and geography lesson.

"You can quote me and I'll say it was all fabricated, that you are a compulsive liar. The job is put on hold. We have some big things happening here, things so big that I can't even tell you. So I notified Dufrene that it'll be next year maybe, but it might not be so long before you can come to work. It depends. You've messed up, son, buying up in Mount Olive. Where you bought it, when you bought it. You got to move on for now. Go on back to Packwood Corners." Roberts leaned forward in his leather swivel chair.

"Wait a second. I just paid good money for that house and land. I can't throw it away and leave," I said.

He went on. "Just put some pressure on the bank, Tadlock, and they'll hand the money back to you. Moxley's important and you need to stay away from him."

"You mean Moxley's on the payroll?"

"I didn't say that. Let's just say he's useful and important to business. This is what you do. Go to your salesman and show him your little letter there. Tell him what happened. Then go over to Tickfaw State Bank and show Logan Smitt. Then tell the both of them that you want your money back or you'll go see T. Roe Shows and that'll be for a good lawsuit. T. Roe'll like the smell of this. All of them at the bank know about Cotton's reputation and that he lives nearby. I hear tell Cotton threatened some of them over at the bank when they repossessed it. Go on and move back down to Packwood Corners. They'll cut you a check soon enough. Bet it won't be thirty days."

"Sheriff Roberts, first, I bought the land and want to have it. Second, what about the job you promised?"

"All things in due course, Tadlock. But don't screw up, you hear?"

"Uh-huh. Sure thing, Sheriff. Sure thing," I said, walking out the door to leave.

I drove to the post office and made four copies of the note and stuck the original in an envelope with a stamp and mailed it to Aunt Cat's box, addressed to my name for safekeeping. I wanted to document the evidence if I could. I was dubious about what might happen, considering how the day was going, and how Moxley was damn sure following me around.

Then I went over to Sam Bullfinch's office to get some quick answers.

Mr. Bullfinch had two clients, porky redheads with pale skin, a man and woman in matching yellow terry-cloth shirts. They looked like brother and sister in some incestuous coupling.

Underneath their shallow talk was the question of whether any undesirables, blacks, lived in a certain Ruthberry subdivision. Mr. Bullfinch assured the couple that they did not and would not ever live there. He lived in the very same development himself, he reminded them.

I waited by the glass doors in the foyer of the building. The room was uncluttered, with several desks lined up like a typing pool, though Bullfinch was the only one working in the room at the time.

When the couple waddled to the door to leave a few minutes later, I went to Mr. Bullfinch's desk and handed him a copy of the note. Then I told him the story of Balem Moxley's threat and about not getting the job.

Sam listened slack-jawed, as if he'd never heard anything like this before, or maybe he was just surprised that it came to a head so soon. I couldn't read his reaction well.

"Did you know anything about this man's claim on the place?" I asked.

He put his hands over his face, like a child playing peek-a-boo.

Right then I knew I'd stepped into a pile of wet cowshit.

"Well," he said, removing his hands, "your property has a clear deed according to the title company and you have title insurance if the man does have a legitimate claim."

"Again, Mr. Bullfinch, did you know anything of Moxley's claim or about his reputation as a bad neighbor?"

"Moxley who?"

"Balem Moxley," I replied.

"Cotton?" he asked. "I've never heard of him before."

The words kind of sunk down deep, all at once. "I never said 'Cotton.'"

He was silent, his face bluish red. He started to apologize and then explained that I'd gotten the deal of the century. He said I should just sell it to someone else and move on.

I stood up in front of his desk and was about one turn from beating the pulp out of him. "Mr. Bullfinch, I want the land I paid cash money for. That was twenty-eight thousand dollars and all my fees, and not one dime less. I want my land and house I paid for in peace. I'm going to see T. Roe Shows about this."

I walked out with no good-byes, walked to my pickup and then over to Tickfaw State Bank, where I waited till lunch for Logan Smitt, the bank president. He never showed, so I was finally sent to the manager for legal claims, a pointy-nose woman with round wire-rimmed glasses named Reitts. Reitts took notes and said that I'd hear from Smitt by the next afternoon. She asked if she could help out with anything.

"Yeah. Go get a damned gun and shoot Balem Moxley between the eyes."

She asked me to leave the bank immediately. I left.

I didn't go see T. Roe Shows, and didn't have any intention to. I went to see another attorney, Ellis Brady, second cousin on my mama's side of the family, a childhood friend. Over at the law office, Ellis said right away that he only handled criminal cases, indigent defense mostly, and domestic stuff. "I defend the monsters," he said, smiling like he does when he wants to shock you. If I didn't get into real trouble, there wasn't much he could do, he said. He explained that by the nature of it all, he thought I needed to get my money back from the bank. The salesman, Bullfinch, may have withheld pertinent information from me and this alone ought to put me on good legal ground. If the bank staff knew Moxley's antics, this, too, would be all the better.

"What else can I do?" I asked. "At this point I want the house and land."

"Jesse, be careful. Start gathering information on Moxley. Know your enemy better than he knows himself. I'll do what I can to look into his past and his present."

"What if the house burns or something?" I asked.

"You don't have insurance, do you?"

"I could get some."

"It'll probably take sixty days to go into effect."

"I might not be fighting this battle that long."

"Jesse, you won't."

At noon I ate lunch alone at the Mighty Chef, a hometown fast-food joint, and drove back up I-12 to Mount Olive. I wasn't sure if Moxley followed me all the way from the house, or if he'd simply been called up by the sheriff and alerted of my appointment. I intended to do some recon and see what the hell to make out of Moxley, see what he was about and what I could uncover.

That afternoon was somewhat calm at the house in Mount Olive, but I couldn't find Johnny. He was missing. I walked the property line where the surveyor had chopped the thickets, and where wooden stakes with red flags were hammered into the ground to point out the boundaries of the ten-acre tract. I carried the .22 magnum rifle and scope, some extra rounds in my pockets. I saw no sign of Johnny or Balem Moxley, and I spent two hours calling the beagle dog's name and looking around. Though new to the place, it wasn't like him to wander off. Mama's dog coming up missing was another great burden I would carry the rest of the evening and into the night.

I went back to the country store and phoned Uncle Red's place. I thought about calling Penny but decided not to because I was low on pocket change for the pay phone. I spoke to my uncle and told him about the whole mess, from the lost job to the note on the windshield to the dog coming up missing.

Uncle Red said that he needed to pick up some crab pots and some nets in the lake that he'd just bought, and he asked me to come with him; maybe we could figure something out. I was to be there at daylight the next morning and this gave me comfort. At least I'd have something to occupy my time.

CHAPTER 9

Johnny was still missing the next morning when I awoke, and I knew he was gone for good. I also believed Moxley had some part in this and was probably creeping around my house and yard when I was down in Ruthberry the day before.

I ate the same breakfast I always eat when I do the cooking, oatmeal, coffee, and milk, and I could feel the presence of my mother in the room with me, dressed in one of her long denim skirts that she made for herself on an electric sewing machine she kept in the spare bedroom. Her hair was long in the mornings before she wrapped it into a tight bun atop her head.

The bills started to arrive for her illness but she never had anything to her name of economic value, so the doctors and hospital pretty soon decided to hunt elsewhere for their pound of flesh. What she left me was an inheritance off-limits from the doctors, thanks to New York Life and the clear statement called beneficiary status. Those doctors soon stopped looking for money to come out from under a rock and moved on. Mama left me the policy and some cheap furniture and that was about it, save a 1973 Plymouth four-door sedan. I'd left the car underneath her rent house carport in case I needed it later.

I arrived at Uncle Red's in time to gather biscuits and pork sausage from Aunt Latrice's table, a snack while fishing. I placed the food in a paper towel.

At Uncle Red's truck, I removed the pistol from the front of my blue jeans and put it on the truck seat. As I rode with him, hauling his skiff to the lake, I ate the contents of the napkin, drinking coffee from a plastic mug, not holding off till dinner.

I thought about Penny and the get-together we had planned for the evening. I remembered how small her waist was in 1977. I remembered her soft skin. We'd made love often at my uncle's deer camp, when no one was around. We made love on the seat of my truck in almost freezing weather, once in the middle of a gravel road, my eyes trained above the seat to watch for cars. Days before I left for the military, she was on her period. I was glad I wasn't leaving part of me behind, though I surely was leaving part of my soul behind.

Uncle Red and I drove down to Pass Tickfaw, the place between Lake Tickfaw and Lake Pontchartrain, where the water was brackish and the surrounding swamp looked like the Florida Everglades. Cypress, much of it dying from saltwater, surrounded the pass and caused the whole flatscape to look like some other world, almost like a science fiction movie on late-night TV. It couldn't be any more different a country from the hills of Mount Olive, though it was all a part of the land called Baxter Parish.

On the way, Uncle Red asked me a few questions about Moxley. I could tell that he was near the point of explosion. I could tell this by the way he moved from sentence to sentence, his voice sharp and quick around each word. I understood he took this attack on my land as a personal insult, and I also knew that it would not go unchallenged.

"You can't wait around on lawyers and bankers and accountants or the law. That ain't our way; it ain't the Tadlock way," Uncle Red said.

"Well—," I tried to talk. I didn't like where he was headed, but I saw where he was going with all of this.

"Well nothing," he said. "Waiting just ain't gonna fly. It ain't how the family does business."

He said no more and I kept quiet. I understood he was telling me the way things had to work, but I questioned if we were headed down the wrong road with the troubles in Mount Olive.

We pulled into the launch at seven. Uncle Red's sixteen-foot fiberglass lake skiff hung on the trailer behind his pickup truck, and five trucks with empty trailers were parked in the oyster shell lot. One beat-up Dodge Dart car was backing a green aluminum bateau and trailer into the watery launch. This was the only free boat launch on this side of the pass, and many fishermen used it daily.

While we waited in the parking lot at the boat launch, Uncle Red reminded me about a man named Palestine Teal in Pickleyville who was a fence for stolen property, weapons of all types, and how the local police protected him for no better reason than he sold them all the munitions they could ever desire, always at a fair price, way cheaper than at the high-dollar Land of Sports downtown. Most Pickleyville cops built their personal arsenals and gun collections through Teal, Uncle Red explained.

"We might have to go see Teal. Teal owes me a favor, and he can get shit done that no white man can get done in the parish," my uncle said.

I knew the men shared a level of respect that went back to the time when my Uncle Roy was alive. He said that Teal might be able to help, even if the Sheriff's Office would not. Teal could get us some weapons.

"Do we really need any more guns? Don't you have enough already?"

"You can't never have enough guns."

I understood what he was saying and did not understand any of it at the same time. I started to say something else but figured it was pointless.

We launched the boat and went through a series of canals near the high-rise interstate and motored far out into Lake Tickfaw, a shallow lake about eight miles wide.

Finally we stopped where Uncle Red thought a gill net might be that he recently purchased for ten dollars from a man named Milton Rogers, who had given up on Louisiana and packed his wife and three kids in a U-Haul and moved to Knoxville for work in a new plant.

I pushed forward to stand in the bow of the boat, steadying myself by gripping both sides of the skiff. I stuck both arms out and took the first halting step toward the bow. It had been a long time since I'd gone out on the lake fishing. I was trying to get my sea legs, pushing down a little nausea into my lower abdomen.

I noticed the deadness on this side of the shallow lake at eight in the morning. Already hot, no one was stirring, no distant outboard motors making noise, no wildlife visible above the water. A dull haze hung across the lake that seemed to cut silence in half and give back nothing.

The buoy Milton told Uncle Red about was easy enough to find, a quarter mile out from the mouth of the Tickfaw River. One hundred yards away was a sapling pole sticking out of the water three feet like an obelisk, blaze orange spray paint to mark it.

The lake was flat as polished glass at that moment, and I was glad for it. There was a tranquility out there, a good distance from the shoreline, the swampy cypress edge. The troubles up in Mount Olive seemed faraway. The morning brought a peace that I wasn't used to, and it made me question why I had gone to Mount Olive, to the hill country, when I could have bought a fish camp on the lake near the parish line and lived this kind of water-bound life.

"Pull the boat over to the pole," Uncle Red said. "That's the one the net's tied to, no doubt."

I stretched out the worn paddle to pull the skiff into the wooden pole. The vertebrae in my back popped from the movement. The pole was dark from algae at the water level, and I got both hands around the pole and started jerking and twisting and tugging till it broke off. I fell when it gave way and kneeled into the skiff's bottom. When the pole snapped, I placed it in the floor of the skiff and the two of us began to retrieve the long net. Uncle Red moved to the center of the skiff and pulled the net taut. I saw the first of the fish, mullet, shad, and alligator gar. Trash fish, mostly dead. We were slow to get them out of the net, trying to save the net from gaps and rips. The monofilament net had wrapped itself bitterly into the fish flesh. As we pulled the fish out we dropped their spotted, sickened or dead corpses into the water.

Milton had warned Uncle Red that the net would contain dead fish. It should have been run a week earlier. Milton sold his boat to pay for the U-Haul rental, and he let Uncle Red have his traps and nets for almost nothing.

Milton was right, I thought, as Uncle Red pried from the net half a rotten catfish whose blue skin had turned pink with decay. I tore a two-foot long gar apart with my bare hands, down to the bone. The dead gar floated at the edge of the boat as if a witness to the waste, food for crabs, as if it and the other dead fish were a testament to all that was wrong in the world, lingering like a blind fool in the morning light.

But the next thing I saw was not a fish; it was unexpected, a brown wood duck wrapped in the net, drowned, buoyancy gone, a dead duck with a limp neck. The bird must have dove in after the fish, I guess. I tried to quiet my stomach by dropping the duck and a handful of net back into the water. I raised myself up from my hunched-over squat and looked toward the west, toward the river.

Uncle Red proclaimed the net was a lost cause. My uncle pulled his Barlow knife from his pocket and began jerking the net up from the water and rip-cutting the fish out of the mesh diamonds with the blade. As he dropped a blue cat into the water, I saw the gaping hole in the net, and then another duck came into view, and before we were done seven more ducks were disinterred from the gill net.

I reached for the Buck knife attached to my belt by a black leather scabbard at my side and started to cut fish out with long slashes, and we cut the rest of the fish out as well and piled the mangled net into the boat.

I crouched back to the stern and looked at the wasted net piled high like the ghostly hairs of a fallen angel in the bow of the skiff. Uncle Red stood over it for a few seconds with a half-pint of Old Crow in his hand. He took a swallow of the whiskey he'd retrieved from his overalls pocket.

We left that place at about ten o'clock. After picking up several fish traps, slat traps that were empty of everything but slimy mud cat, Uncle Red made three pulls on the motor's rope crank and pointed the skiff back toward the canal and home.

We boated through the interstate canal that led to the launch. On the way back from the pass, near the concrete I-55 high-rise above the swamp, I saw something moving in the cattails near the water. We were going slow because one side of the canal had camps for trappers and commercial fishermen; it was a no-wake zone and we puttered through. I thought it might be a whitetail deer or something wild at first, or maybe a feral hog, but as we got closer I saw that it looked like a man. I was sitting at the bow of the skiff watching for logs that some-times floated up to the surface of the water, the kind of obstruction that could ruin a lower unit on an outboard engine.

Again, I saw the standing image in the brush. I could see that it was a person, a human. I began to point. It looked like a man in a cowboy hat. It looked like Moxley. Then it disappeared, and the cattails quit moving. I began motioning all the more for Uncle Red to stop. He did begin to stop the boat. The noise from the boat motor and the cars chuck-chuck-chunking across the spans of the interstate bridge to our east made it hard to communicate while the boat moved. I felt sure it was Moxley.

Uncle Red slowed the engine, placing it in neutral.

"I think I saw a man over there on the bank. It looked like Moxley."

My uncle shrugged his shoulders indicating that perhaps I was just seeing things. "I didn't see nothing."

"All right," I said.

When we got started again, the apparition never reappeared. It reminded me of the time I shot at a rabbit in a briar patch. Johnny's mama was among the beagle dogs hunting in the back field at Uncle Red's. I shot at a slip rabbit, one I saw running, but not a rabbit pursued by the hounds. After I fired, I looked for the rabbit but I apparently missed. Then I started calling the dogs and they came about five minutes later, and my cousin Russ came, too, and the dogs found no trail at all. The hounds never barked. It was as if I'd witnessed a ghost and the ghost didn't leave a scent for the dogs to pursue. Russ questioned me and shrugged his shoulders exactly the way Uncle Red raised his out on the water, a feeling of doubt expressed without saying a word.

"You sure you seen something?" he hollered, his voice trying to overcome the hum of the motor as we started off again.

"I saw it. I saw Moxley and you're just going to have to trust me on that. I know I saw him."

When we got back to the boat launch a few minutes later, I could see no signs of the man or his ghost. We tied the boat to the wood pier, the air smelling of rotten crabs, the stench hitting me in the face. The stinging June wind brought a garbage smell to the boat.

I walked down the creosote bulkhead toward the truck, Uncle Red's key ring in my palm, the revolver in my waistband. Nobody was at the launch, and there were only two trucks with trailers parked in the parking lot. One white Dodge pickup obscured Uncle Red's vehicle from view, though it was only seventy-five feet away. When I got to Uncle Red's Ford truck I saw that it was sitting on the rims, the tires flat like rolls of rubber on the ground. They were busted of air. The first tire and then the second tire. I walked around the truck. All four tires were flat and the hood was cracked open about three inches, as if someone had taken liberty with the contents of the motor.

A little warning was set on top of the air cleaner, a handwritten note penned in big black letters: "24 HOURS TO GET THE HELL OUT OF MOUNT OLIVE OR MEET HELL ITSELF," read the message.

My uncle was livid at first. He drank the rest of the whiskey and shattered the bottle against the side panel of the truck. Then he leaned his elbows against the toolbox and smoked a few Camels till he calmed down.

I walked a half mile to the pass, to the little fishing village named Reno, and I called the law at a clapboard bait shop. Later two sheriff's deputies took a report and dusted for fingerprints. The battery was stolen in addition to the tires being slashed.

There wasn't a clear print anywhere. Nothing. They radioed a tire man.

Uncle Red was controlling his temper more than I figured he would. I could tell there was a reason for it, some good reason. I carried on and on about the trouble in Mount Olive and with the Sheriff's

Office till I saw Uncle Red's hard gaze. He meant for me to get quiet fast.

It was already one o'clock by the time we got through with road service. We got retreads from the tire man, along with air, and mounting; he charged two hundred and thirty bucks for the tires and service call.

We got back on the highway. "You need to keep your mouth shut," Uncle Red said.

"I've been messed over and now you. Last thing we need to do is keep quiet. Hell, Moxley's following us."

"I questioned you out yonder on the canal but no more," Uncle Red said.

"Yes sir."

"You keep your mouth shut cause that son of a bitch is above the law. It's about time we go below the goddamned law."

As we drove north into the heart of Baxter Parish, I remembered something one of the deputies said. He was a Hart boy from Pickleyville that I knew from back in high school. He was about to get into his Crown Vic cruiser and drive away, having done nothing much at all to help us except for calling the tire man; I followed him to his car. I made it clear that I had been screwed all the way around.

The Hart boy's words cut me. It sounded strange at the moment, but I worked it around in my head. The deputy looked me in the eye. "Great to see you've made it back home, old friend," he laughed. "Jesse, welcome to the fallen paradise."

CHAPTER 10

Uncle Red was sullen when we unhitched the skiff from the back bumper of his truck. We were underneath a sycamore tree in his yard where he always kept the boat. When he opened his mouth I knew to listen.

"This feller Moxley is like a gift," he said without looking up from where he was wrapping the iron safety chains around the tongue of the trailer hitch. "He's a free gift in a way I don't like. What's got to be done is to unwrap the gift, and it ain't going to be nothing nice. It's going to hurt like hell, but the gift is a-waiting."

I knew what he meant. I knew he meant there would be bloodshed or cowardice. That was the gift: a test. The only way to disprove cowardice is to face your own bloodshed, he'd told me many times before.

"So, what do we do?" I asked, the pain running up my chest to my jaws and throat.

"Face him on our own terms. Make him come to us and show hisself. Cut off the snake's head when he pokes it out from the hole."

An hour later we drove to an out-of-the-way section of Pickleyville a few blocks from the mansions on Thomas Jefferson Avenue, west of the downtown, just a few blocks off the main streets where the city's signature houses of wealth and power stood in a paternal watch. Everything transformed into slums like the barrios I saw in San Juan, Puerto Rico, in the Army, when I was there in 1985. Out of sight from the good white people of Pickleyville were old-time servants' quarters and the housing projects, a section the inhabitants called the Third World.

On Washington Street, black men stood on the sidewalks dealing crack. A grown man without a shirt tooled around on a pink girls bicycle. Wrecked cars littered the dirt yards, and hulls of houses looked worse than the homes in Puerto Rico. Women and men stared at us from the porches and stoops of rotting-down shacks.

In the rear of a washeteria sat Mr. Palestine Teal, a bald man the color of a cheap cigar, tobacco brown. The man's shoulders were slumped a little, as if he would one day, in old age, become completely hunchbacked with arthritis. He sat in front of a desktop made of plywood nailed across two wooden sawhorses. Teal sat deep in a plush chair. Two other men sat on plastic five-gallon oil buckets in the unadorned storage room office.

"You Red's brother?" he asked me as I entered the room with Uncle Red.

"No. His nephew."

Uncle Red grunted.

Teal motioned for the other men to leave, and they walked through the door. "You gots a problem?"

"A little. We need some friends."

"How many and what kind?"

"A M1 Garand .30-06, a M16 full auto, a couple of .45 Colts like we used in Korea, but brand-new, no worn-out shit. Some boxes of ammunition, four boxes of .30-06 rounds, four .223s, and ten boxes of rounds for .45 pistols. Some two-inch pull-type polyurethane detonators to put on them kind of dogs that bark real loud and bite real hard," Uncle Red said to the man.

Teal took a draw off of a long joint stuck in a roach clip. The smell was sweet and strong, filling the cinder block room.

"Let me just keep the .38. No need for a Colt," I said.

"Suit yourself," said Uncle Red.

Teal made some marks on a piece of brown paper bag with a pencil. "Eight for all of them friends. The caps is hard to get, what costs the most. How many?"

"Twenty-five. That's kind of steep," Uncle Red said.

"Costs to do business in this town, all the people you got to keep happy on the city council, black and white. They all wants they donations. You try getting dynamite caps anywhere around here. Play like hell doing it. Them caps cost you a extra hundred."

"All right. I'll also pay for some information on a feller up in the north end of the parish at Mount Olive. I want to know how he does what he does without trouble coming from the sheriff? Why's he so damned tight with the sheriff? What might take him down? Name's Balem Moxley. Some call him Cotton."

"No charge for information. Truth be free like air."

"All right," Uncle Red told him.

Teal's face tensed as if he weighed his words, his yellow-white eyes wide around coal-colored pupils. "If you wants it, meets me at the parking lot of the Lutheran's church by the college baseball field, tomorrow at noon. Be alone. Just the two of you mens." He smiled a mouthful of bright teeth.

We left.

"You got a choice," Uncle Red said once we got back in the pickup. "You either do what I tell you, what's got to be done, or you leave the place up yonder. Get you a lawyer and sue, but never go back. We don't have to meet Teal tomorrow. He'll sell the stuff to somebody else. If we go, we're going to use it. What do you want?"

"I don't know. Take the bastard's head off. Or get the hell back in the Army. I really don't know."

"Be sure you know by in the morning, cause we got to set the wheel in motion. Know by the morning what we gonna do with Balem Moxley."

Through some phone calls to men familiar with the north end of the parish, friends who hunted deer and fox with Carlin in a hunting club on the south end and up in Mississippi at the Homochitto National Forest near Natchez, I heard several stories about Moxley. One hunter told me that Cotton Moxley was a federal marshal, others said he was A.T.F.; a few said he was an undercover deputy sheriff. They mentioned that he had a trade, that he was indeed an electrician, but he mostly traveled the country in a van and fought dogs, sometimes roosters. He often drove an old Harley-Davidson with a little leather bicycle seat.

A chicken farmer echoed the words of the country store owner: Cotton Moxley was a lifelong hog and cattle rustler. He said Moxley had been a stock thief since the age of eleven or twelve. Several mentioned his poaching of wild game and his breeding of some of the meanest and biggest bulldogs in the South, a crossbred strain of giant bulldogs mixed with the mastiffs of the Canary Islands and white Argentine bulldogs. Thus, his own make and model of one-hundred-twenty pounders, many trained to attack on command. Another guy said the dog business alone could make him rich, but Moxley used dope and spent every penny that he made on it. He also said that Moxley was an arsonist from childhood, and rumor had it Moxley burned houses for the sheriff when need be.

As I knew already, Moxley was married and had one kid at least, maybe more. His wife was a naturally beautiful woman, but in such a hard and worn out sort of way not to make her very tempting.

As I understood it, Moxley had whores in every community up and down Baxter Parish, and despite his looks, he spread his seed often. He was a ghoul, a freak. The man hardly ever bathed, one hunter said, and yet it seemed as though he carried with him a charisma impossible to comprehend.

I learned that Moxley was gone much of the year, weeks at a time, in his van with kennels on a trailer and his canine exercise equipment, a treadmill, a spinning jenny, all for training dogs while on the road.

He ran a kind of mobile operation that could appear out of nowhere, and he had within him some kind of skill or gift or power that made him able to emerge, as if dropped down amidst a place he could not have walked to or driven. He was an enigma and a mystery. A couple men said they'd watched him appear in the swamps as far east as Picayune, Mississippi, and as far north as the National Forest at a place called Union Church near the Mississippi River.

Every tale agreed on a couple of points: he was dangerous and was protected by local law enforcement. Most of the men spoke of run-ins with Moxley, mostly by way of local legend. Every one of them expressed a level of fear and caution in dealing with him.

I'd brought a change of clean clothes, blue jeans, and a pullover polo shirt when I left that morning, knowing there were consequences to this kind of trouble. A man ought to be prepared. I had put Penny off long enough, from the time I'd seen her at Mama's after the funeral. I didn't think she'd stand for much more delay.

After making myself presentable at Aunt Cat's, I went to see Penny at her house. It was almost seven o'clock when I arrived.

"I want to talk a minute, Jesse," Penny said as I walked into the cypress cottage.

"Sure. All right."

We sat down on her couch, a full seat's width between us. There was a smell of scented candles that were especially feminine, very feminine.

I was uneasy all of a sudden, as uneasy as when I saw the monster with a gun in my yard. It was like I was about to be called down for something.

"I'm a little anxious about the two of us. What are your intentions?" she asked.

"Well—"

She interrupted me at midsentence. "I need to know if you plan on running away again. I don't have parents anymore, and I don't have anyone to speak up for me." She twisted a sapphire ring around and around on her right ring finger to the point of distraction.

She went on, "Because I don't want to get involved with you if you are about to make a quick exit." She stared at me with a vast and deep intensity that I wasn't used to.

"I have no exit plan. I don't have any plans to leave." I was ashamed, riddled with hopes for a way out.

"That's not good enough. I'm thirty years old and divorced. My husband left me to go to medical school. He said I was getting in the way of his future."

"I'm back home for good. You're real important to me, always have been."

She laughed a kind of ironic laugh. "Yes, and you left for the Army. I never stopped wanting to see you, but I don't care to watch you run off again. I need to know that you've changed."

"That was twelve years ago."

"Uh-huh."

"I was a boy a dozen years back. Of course I've changed." I made a bold move and eased down to her end of the couch and kissed her, squeezing her as I did this, holding her in earnest. Penny was soft underneath the blouse, and she gave no resistance to my touch. She held me tightly, gripping my side as we kissed each other.

This went on past the time of the movie. We left for the theater oblivious to the hour, rode over to the show near the college, the twin cinema, her seated close beside me in the truck, my gun in the glove box next to the handcuffs and flashlight.

Nostalgia had me. All of it, the past filled with glorious events that never really happened between Penny and me. We were just kids when I left.

Penny's face had changed, her cheeks rounder, her hips full. Her hands were reddish in tint, and nails short and lacquered with clear polish. She was stronger, more of a woman than what I had left behind. She was more attractive to me than ever before.

The movie was already started when we walked up to the ticket window.

"Where to now?" she asked.

"How about Graziano's Seafood for supper?"

She said yes.

Over at Graziano's, we ate several pounds of boiled crawfish and fried softshell crabs and golden brown hushpuppies. We drank a few beers between us and enjoyed jokes and laughter and funny stories while we sucked the salty wet juice from the crawfish heads.

Penny talked about her work in ER and about the sometimes-gruesome abuse of children, the hardest part of what she dealt with on a daily basis. I learned more about her life in Texas, the missing years while we were apart.

I told her about my time in the Army, and she listened carefully, as if she wanted to judge what had become of me, if I had indeed changed. What, if anything at all, had made me different from 1977?

After I paid the bill, we went to her house, smelling of beer and seafood.

"Do you think your mother's dog is going to turn up?" she asked, sitting back on her couch.

My stomach was bloated from the food and the aftereffects of beer. "No," I said. "I think he's long gone and I doubt I'll ever see hide nor hair of him again, but I'd like to know what happened to him for certain."

"That's just terrible. Your mother loved that little dog. "

"Yeah, it's bad."

"What do you plan to do with your life, Jesse?" she rubbed her hand across my forearm lightly.

"I came home to stay. I thought when I came home that I had a job and money enough for a house. Seems I have neither. You're about the only thing left that I hoped to come home to."

"Don't mess around. If you want me, it's going to take some work." She showed me the door. I kissed her good night and left for Mount Olive.

I drove alone, thinking the whole way about fighting the bank. Maybe re-upping and joining the Army. Maybe getting out a highway map of the United States and driving off to places unknown. Maybe out West. Maybe I could find Wyoming or Montana if I tried hard enough to leave this place. I was also thinking about Penny and what all this trouble meant for us. I could see her being pulled into my troubles, and this made me want to leave all the more.

When I got back to the darkened house on the state line, I called for Johnny. It was already far into the night. He didn't come, no sign of him being there at all except for some uneaten dog food in a ceramic bowl on the porch. This was the only reminder that he was ever there. I hurt for the dog. I hurt and wished like hell he'd come home all right.

CHAPTER 11

Throughout the night I lay in my bed sweating, the window unit not working, probably low on coolant, the box fan in the other window spinning, blowing around the wet heat.

I spent more than a decade of the most boring years possible in the U.S. Army. During the cold war, with covert operations across the globe, the action was zero. I saw no war between 1977–1989, even with Ronald Reagan's constant saber-rattling. We were an all-volunteer Army, transformed from weakness to perceived strength, though I believe the draft had done something all-volunteers could not do: offer creativity. We had little. We had a job and we were employees. I was in Supply, the most boring of all Army work.

I understood how Uncle Red felt about the Army, how they told you where to shit, when to shit, and how to shit, where to bury your shit. How you had no freedom while defending freedom.

I had a dozen years to think about what might have occurred if I'd told Principal Herrin to go take a walk in hell, and then let my uncle do to battle when they tried to expel me.

Undoubtedly, I would have gotten Penny Nesom pregnant and married her right away, taken some kind of job in a chemical plant or stayed in Packwood Corners and worked around Pickleyville.

In bed, I was trying hard to go to sleep, but my mind took me to a place as far away from north Baxter Parish as China. I'd grown up in the south end of the parish and never ventured very far from it till I enlisted. How thirty miles due south from where I lay could be a different world, I did not know. I was out of place in Mount Olive and I could feel it in the sinews of my bones. It was as distant as the Black Forest, or Japan, or Puerto Rico, places the service took me.

The fan hummed and walloped into the night. I figured that Moxley might be lurking in the briar thickets with his gun and with the great big dog named Saul.

I got up out of the bed and went into the wood-walled kitchen for something to drink. At the refrigerator, I drained the last of the sweet tea, emptied it with a few swallows, turned off the lights and went back to bed. The house, Sam Bullfinch said, was built in 1895. A long time ago, I thought. My mama wouldn't have wanted me to lose my money on this house. She would want me to fight harder for the piece of land than I would have fought for my own country. Mama would claw and fight, leaving bloody marks cut into Moxley's flesh and whoever else got in the way. Skin would be underneath her fingernails from the battle.

"Let them know you was there," she'd say. "Let them that cause you trouble know you was birthed in this world too."

Still unable to sleep, I turned on the lamp at my nightstand. It let me see the whiteness of my freckled skin. In the Army, the long sleeves I wore kept me pale. Always a lack of sun. The hair was thin and reddish on my forearms. I picked up a book off the nightstand, a history of the J.F.K. assassination written by a local teacher at the junior college, and I read it till I went groggy-eyed.

The next morning, I awoke in a start at five o'clock. There was a noise outside and I reached for the revolver on the nightstand. Right then I knew the seventy-two hours had passed without even thinking. The gun was loaded with six hollow point bullets, one hundred fifty grains apiece.

I lay there without breathing, listening to the fan spin. After a moment, I slid out of bed and eased down the center hall of the house to the front door. I quietly turned the knob. I'll never forget the lack of sound.

I opened the door fast, jerking it open, and then I unlatched the screen door and gave it a quick shove.

I could see a form, a lump on the edge of the porch, all the way over at the steps six feet away from where I stood.

My head flooded with pain, intuition telling me what I was seeing almost before I even saw it. I flicked on the light switch and the darkness fled.

It was a ball of hairy meat, dried blood and flesh. I knew it was Johnny as my eyes adjusted to the porch lights.

It could have been a mound of cheap meat. It could have been a big coon hit on the road, dragged below a sports car a few miles. Or it could have been some wild dead thing, as wild things meet the hardness of a cruel world often times.

But it was a dog. That was sure enough. I took two steps. My stomach got even more taut. I got closer and could smell death. Bone was exposed in spots. The brown markings looked like Johnny's coat. It appeared jabbed with a metal rod, an ice pick no doubt. The hair remaining on the dog was matted, full of proud red flesh. Dead meat. I could see enamel white canines at one end, bared, the lips ripped off, teeth razor-edged on a broken, disjointed jawbone.

There was a note stuck to the dog's ribcage with a wood-handled ice pick. I reached down and tore the note off, leaving the ice pick in the animal. The blood had started to seep through and smudge the ink. I went back into the hall under the light to read, unsure if Moxley was gone from the yard.

YOUR TIME IS UP. I WARNED YOU. YOUR LITTLE DOG WAS

ALIVE. I TORTURED HIS LITTLE ASS. SWEET LITTLE RUNT JUST LIKE YOU. ALIVE PLENTY TILL I GOT A HOLD OF HIM. HE SQUEALED LIKE YOU WILL. TADLOCK STAY IN MOUNT OLIVE AND DIE LIKE A DOG.

At that moment and the moments afterward I regretted ever coming to the place. My mother loved that dog. He slept in her bed. He was always at her feet. This was no kind of existence for the owner of his first house. There was a pain of ownership, not pride, and I wished right then and there that I was still in the Army half a world away.

I slammed the door and put on a pair of blue jeans and a brown Army T-shirt. I stuck the pistol in my belt at my back and laced up a pair of combat boots. I went out on the porch, then to the carport, and backed the pickup to the front door.

I loaded the dog, or tried to load him in the bed of the truck, a plastic garbage bag wrapped around each of my hands like gloves. I gripped the dog's front and back leg with a hand on each and lifted, but the front leg broke off as I picked the animal up, and it fell back to the ground with a thud. I tried the other front leg and finally got Johnny up on the tailgate. Then I placed the severed leg beside the corpse.

Dry heaves attacked my chest, my nerves still shot with anger. The smell of death engulfed the porch.

I was soon heading west on Highway 38 toward downtown Mount Olive before daylight, the pistol on the seat, driving someplace else, though I didn't know where.

CHAPTER 12

The first place I went after finding the dog was to my cousin Ellis's law office. It was six-thirty when I got to Ruthberry, ten miles south of Mount Olive. Through the weakening of my rage, I finally realized I was way too early to see any lawyer at work. So I drove out east of town to Duncan Avenue to the rambling antebellum home where Ellis has lived just about his entire life.

I pulled into the gravel drive between the line of dueling cedar trees. I banged on the front door and he came to the screen porch dressed in yellow pajamas, top and bottom like a kid might sleep in. His face looked rough, as if he hadn't shaved in days.

"Jesse, what the hell?"

"Moxley's killed Mama's dog. He left him on the porch. Yesterday, the son of a bitch followed me, cut Uncle Red's truck tires. I got to do something. He's cost me a job. I got the dog in the bed of the truck. The beagle dog looks like hamburger meat."

He scratched his chin and opened the screen door for me to come inside.

"I didn't wake the wife and kids, did I?"

"Oh, man. We divorced a year ago. I got a lawyer's life. No good for a woman and children. Now they just get my fat check once a month when I send it."

We went into his study, a sort of at-home law office, legal books wall-to-ceiling. I relayed to Ellis all of the information I'd gleaned from the hunters. I asked him if he'd found out anything for me yet on Moxley.

"Of course not," he said. "But I'll go see Judge Marshall about a temporary restraining order today. He'll grant it. Marshall doesn't like anybody, especially the sheriff. If Moxley comes near you, within one hundred feet, he'll get himself arrested. That's step one, but we got to do a hell of a lot more."

"What?"

"There are crazies in the world, Jesse. Stark-raving nutsoids. I've known some of them, represented a bunch of them. Some for murder. Not one got the chair under my counsel. What we need right now is information, information that leads to knowledge. Does Moxley smoke crack? Does he pay his taxes? How did he kill the dog? Where? When? Has he ever been arrested before? If so, why was he arrested? What's his connection to Haltom Roberts and Felix Dufrene? Leaving the handwritten notes might be his big mistake. We need to answer this stuff fast," Ellis said.

"I'm game."

"OK. Let's go see the dog. I've got a theory about the dog."

Ellis put on a pair of leather house slippers, and we went out into the yard, it barely daylight. He took pictures of Johnny in the back of the truck with a 35-millimeter camera. He poked on the dog's mangled flesh with a limb.

A mocking bird chased a big blue jay across the yard in the pitch of battle. I automatically ducked without thinking, and Ellis ducked his head too.

"You said Moxley has bulldogs?"

"Uh-huh. Damned hundred-pounders."

Ellis washed his hand across his nose. "One time, when I was just a kid, our yellow Labrador retriever came up missing. He was a good dog and he loved everybody; anybody could catch him. He'd been gone a day or two. I put reward flyers up and down Duncan Avenue, rode my bike all the way up to the tracks on Highway 16. Even talked to the chief of police about my missing pet.

"Then on the way back home I saw something lying in the ditch on Harrell Road right up from the house here, across the creek. It looked like a goat carved up ready for the spit. I stopped my bike and took a closer inspection. It was Old Rocky, cut up just like this dog of yours.

"Daddy started asking around; pretty quick he found out that Turnish Wincher, a new neighbor over across the creek, used common dogs to train his pit bulls to fight. He'd tie the dog in a yard and turn out bulldogs on him until he was dead. Old Rocky was near their house."

"What did your old man do?" I asked.

"Nothing. Daddy didn't do a thing. Soon another dog came up missing. Then another dog in the neighborhood. Then another. Sometimes Turnish would drop the dog off where he found it, usually in a ditch within a few feet from where he lured it to his truck with bacon strips, dropping off the dead dog was kind of a calling card."

"Goddamned bastard."

"Yeah, but finally daddy put a stop to it."

"How?"

"Well, it's sort of funny thing. Daddy said for me to get in the truck. He warned me never to say a word about what was going to happen. I've never told the story until now. Daddy stole the dog of the baddest son of a bitch in Ruthberry, Erlin Snipes. Erlin was the foreman at the oyster shucking plant. The only non-dago foreman that could get along working for the Mob over there. Daddy dropped Erlin's dog off in Turnish's yard a couple of hours before Turnish came home from work. The dog was a Catahoula Erlin called Buddy, the dog Erlin loved like a child. You'd see Erlin all over town with that cur dog up in the cab of the truck, dog's head poked out the window.

"I knew what was happening. I saw what Daddy was doing that day. So I climbed into our tree house at the creek bank to watch the show, a good place to watch the action over in the neighbor's yard.

"Turnish caught the cur dog and tied him to a steel pole with about twenty feet of rope. Then he put a bulldog on the cur. You know we're close to Turnish's place and you could hear the dog go to screaming. You could see from our tall tree house, too. Daddy drove to the pay phone over at B. Stern's Department Store in town and called Erlin up and told him that Turnish Wincher had his dog and was torturing it. Daddy just gave the address, no name."

"I can imagine."

"Don't imagine, Jesse. I'll tell you. Erlin Snipes drove up. You could hear his rattletrap, rusty-mufflered truck through the pines. That truck revved as it stopped in Turnish's yard, the engine dying down all of a sudden. Erlin got out of the truck, shirt off, the cur dog already stone-ass dead, a red-nosed pit bull with his jaws locked hanging onto the throat of the cur like a crab in a net stuck to a chicken leg.

"I couldn't see them at the moment because of the branches and leaves of a tree, but I started hearing another sound. Erlin Snipes beating Turnish with a length of logging chain, dog chain he must of picked up off the ground. Turnish made sounds few white men have ever uttered. He would come in and out of view as he was trying like hell to crawl away from Erlin.

"It was the damnedest thing. Erlin Snipes would beat Turnish a while, then he'd choke him some, then he'd beat him some more. Then Erlin must have realized his cur dog was dead, because he really went berserk. He chained Turnish to the back of his truck and dragged him by his left leg around the pasture in front of the house. Turnish's body would bounce off of ruts in the ground. This lasted about ten minutes.

"I watched all I could. My daddy was laughing his ass off over on the steps of this very house, drinking bourbon. Laughter. Laughter on account of the way his boys cried when they found their dog in the ditch. Laughter at how there's justice that isn't blind sometimes. There's justice that comes out seeing the truth."

I nodded. "What do I do?"

"Out-badass the badass. Kick his nut sack up until his balls are like little gold ringlets around his earlobes."

There was a pause, and the story was washing itself through my brain. "What ever happened to Snipes and Turnish?"

"Well, Turnish lived to a ripe old age, one legged. His left leg had to be removed."

"And Snipes, he got jail?"

"Hell no. He was bailed out the next day. Erlin Snipes died six weeks later in an accident at the oyster plant. A bulldozer fell over on top of him when he was trying to load it on a trailer. He got in a hurry and went forward up the trailer instead of backward and it fell over on him, a freak accident. The thing never went to trial."

Before I left, my cousin said he'd see Judge Marshall and that he would do some research on Moxley. He called the Humane Society in New Orleans and they said to send pictures of Johnny and write them a letter. He kept the bloody note that was ice-picked to the dog and made a copy of it on the Xerox machine in his study. He said he'd draft a quick letter that afternoon to the people in New Orleans. He told me to be careful and keep him updated. There might be more he could do later.

We were standing at my pickup and I was about to leave.

"One more thing, Ellis. Is all this going to be taken care of legally?" I asked.

"I doubt it," he said. "Nothing very important ever is."

The morning sun was burning my eyes. I put on a pair flight glasses I'd bought at a P.X. years ago, sunglasses with scratches on the lenses that nearly made it impossible to see. I drove to Pickleyville and Packwood Corners and pulled into Uncle Red's driveway.

When Uncle Red saw the dog, he asked me to take a ride with him. First, we dug a small hole for Johnny in Uncle Red's yard behind the shop, burying him, then we drove to the meeting point to see Teal. I knew there would be no turning back once we had the meeting, and that scared the hell out of me.

Uncle Red didn't say a word, his lips pursed and dry. He occasionally lit an unfiltered Camel while driving. He would take three or four draws and thump it out the window, the cigarette burned down to a nub at his fingertips.

My uncle wore a white dress shirt that was a little snug in the shoulders and neck and a pair of slick dress trousers, which meant he'd probably been to the union hall or to see a banker earlier in the day, which made me speculate that he'd borrowed the money to buy the weapons. He only dressed this way on special occasions.

Out of the blue he grabbed my shoulder, there in his Ford, with his hand coming from the back of the seat where he'd stretched out his arm. "You know what is done today is more important than secrets in the Army. You understand this is about blood kin? It needs to stay quiet and it ought to be secure. Top secret and off-limits."

"Uh-huh."

"Then let it be kept quiet. You don't know nothing of what happens from here on out, ain't got no recollection of it."

We went past a barroom called Pay Day Someday on U.S. Highway 190 and stopped at the red light crossroads in the heart of town, Dead Man's Curb, there near the Hard-Row. We stayed straight, through the light, and turned left away from the Freeman's Quarters till we came to the railroad tracks. Then we were at St. John's Lutheran Church by the junior college. We hadn't come to a complete stop when Teal pulled in behind us in a dark green Suburban with polished aluminum wheels.

Uncle Red and Teal didn't shake hands. My uncle handed him a thick Levi Garrett chewing tobacco pouch.

Teal put the tan pouch into his back pants pocket without opening it. "I know it'll be right. Better be right," the man said. He opened the door of his Suburban and lifted a golf bag out of it, the end covered in black plastic. It looked heavy by the way he strained when lifting it.

"Be wise. Don't let them caps get dangerous on you." He smiled and two gold teeth caught the sunlight.

Uncle Red stood toe to toe with Teal for a second. "What about the information on Moxley and Roberts?"

"Be to you when I gets it. It takes time."

"We'll be waiting on it."

"I knows you will, Red."

Across town, the Hard-Row was full for a noon crowd. It's where the underbelly of Pickleyville hangs out for beer and barbeque. Uncle Red took his five beef and I ordered two pork sandwiches, and we settled in, standing at the long Formica bar like everyone else crowding the front of the room, the tables in the dining area sparsely populated with men and women eating and reading the newspaper. Two men took their meals outside to eat on the concrete patio furniture.

It occurred to me that forty feet from where we stood, behind

Uncle Red's truck seat, were enough weapons, pistols, high-powered rifles, all stolen as hell, to land both of us in jail for a dozen years, not to mention the bomb detonators. I ate nervously.

The gray-haired woman Celeste grabbed my arm and squeezed it across the bar. She leaned into me. "You keeping that man next to you honest?"

"I'm trying," I said, looking into her faded eyes.

"Honest?" Uncle Red said. "I ain't never been honest."

An old man to my right side broke into the conversation. "Celeste, I'd like nothing more than to be the man that keeps you honest." He grinned over his draft beer.

"Huh, I got two boyfriends already, one named Smitty and the other named Wesson, the both of them right here under this bar. They say you ain't gonna get a chance to keep me nothing." She grimaced. Men snickered at the bar.

The man crushed his cigarette on the table's edge and walked out the room quietly. Nobody cared to tell him good-bye.

"He likes his coffee brown, that Frankie do. But I'm old enough to know better," Celeste said loud so we all could hear.

We drove to Kmart and bought a couple of spools of fishing line and some rolls of stainless steel wire used for making liters to catch alligator gar. Uncle Red loaded a bag of charcoal into the buggy as well.

I knew better than to ask any questions of Uncle Red. He was to be trusted and that was enough. He was about the only one, save my two aunts and perhaps Penny, on my side at this point in the Mount Olive war. I walked out to the truck pushing the buggy while he kept his hands in his overalls pockets.

After leaving the store, Uncle Red purchased a strange assortment of misshapen pipes, bent and rusty lengths of galvanized pipe, from a bargain rack outside the Pickleyville Feed and Farm.

It occurred to me as we left the feed store that I was on the edge of something that might mark me forever. I also realized that there were two kinds of weapons: Those made of flesh, fists, and teeth, and those made by flesh itself. In either case, they killed and maimed without much hesitation or control. They were to be used, and this, by God, was the cost of a little piece of land. I'd learned through reading history that world wars have been fought, more or less, for exactly the same thing. Dirt.

CHAPTER 13

The evening dinner at Aunt Cat's house left me feeling like it was a last meal. My aunts' faces were full of anger over what happened to me and for what happened to Mama's dog. The women hadn't seen the anonymous notes, but they were already angry because in their female ways of knowing, they knew we were withholding things from them.

I sat at the table, a table too big for a childless widow of nineteen years. Aunt Cat kept this big table, I suppose—bought new in downtown Pickleyville at Roland's Furniture on time without interest for a year—because of those who had eaten there, those who were no longer alive. The kitchen table was an object of memory and a place of service.

Despite the gloom, the food was well prepared. Plenty of white beans and sausage with black pepper on rice, but it tasted bland to me. My chest was tight. If I didn't know better, I'd figured it was the warning sign of a heart attack.

"I just wish you would have bought your Mama's house from us," Aunt Latrice said. "We might have sold it to you. Or just kept renting it like she did, and not ventured up to Mount Olive."

Uncle Red ate without saying much, eating with his fork and a slice of bread.

"It's not too late, Jesse, to come on back to Packwood Corners," said Aunt Cat. "You could sell the place up there and let someone else have the headache."

"It's too damn late Cat," Uncle Red remarked, steady scooping beans onto the fork with the bread.

I pushed away my half-eaten plate. "No, I have this to deal with and I've to do what's right. I have to address it."

Uncle Red spoke again, "It's something that's long been in need of doing and it's gonna be done."

Aunt Cat looked away.

"Cat, pass me the sausage bowl. I want some meat," my uncle said.

That evening I went with Uncle Red to his shop behind his house. We cut up lengths of pipe a foot long with a pipe cutter, making a succession of rings around the metal till they broke. Then we cut threads on each end to screw on plugs that he'd placed in a wooden box that looked like a crate. It was two-inch pipe, the ends cut. I screwed on the ends to a dozen pipes. I didn't think about what they would be used for, or what damage they might cause. They were simply pipes. Their purpose was irrelevant. I had sweat on my face and I wiped my neck and cheeks with a rag from the workbench. I went to the door for some air.

"You leaving?" Uncle Red asked.

"No. It's hot as hell in here."

"We ain't got long," he said.

Uncle Red mixed sulfur and saltpeter and charcoal into a fine black powder. Occasionally he'd go outside and light a teaspoonful in a pan and comment on its volatility. He did this like he had done it daily for many years, as if it was utterly routine. When the mix made a sucking sound as he threw in a match, and it flashed fire that burned hair on his arm before he could get away, he said it was almost ready.

From a glass medicine bottle, Uncle Red administered what he called an accelerator. I didn't ask what it was nor did he offer. He placed a half-teaspoon in another pan of gunpowder, the white dust mixed thoroughly. When he got ready to light this one, he told me to step back, and he lit it with a match duct-taped to the end of a cane pole from six feet away.

Cah-boosh! Orange fire leapt five feet and it blew a hole in the plywood table and nearly disintegrated the pan. It scared the hell out of me. My ears rang and my uncle grinned, happy with himself over what he'd just accomplished.

"Brother boy, that's sweet to me," he said.

Aunt Latrice screamed from the back patio, asking what in the world was going on at the shop. We didn't answer.

For an hour or two we packed the pipes with the powder, making it as tight as possible, tamping it down into the pipes with a wooden rod. We used a wadding of newspaper on one end and sealed it with wax, a hole stuck through it for the detonator caps to attach. Then we screwed down the end pieces with holes drilled in them to allow the detonator caps to fuse. I was careful because I knew that a spark could take us and the shack into an orange fireball.

Before this day I had never made a bomb, and it cut a definite imprint upon my soul, the kind of knowledge that keeps a place in your mind forever.

"It's enough for one night," Uncle Red said, as he put two-dozen pipes into a wooden bin, the polyurethane nubs sticking out, the actual caps for the detonators not yet attached to their polyurethane settings.

I knew it was enough, but what does that mean anyway, enough? Enough to kill or be killed, enough to maim or be maimed. I knew Uncle Red was going a few notches across the line of sanity, a few bubbles closer to popping, and this bothered me a lot.

*

I tried to sleep that night at Uncle Red and Aunt Latrice's house. The house where Mama had lived was empty of beds and other furniture I'd taken to Mount Olive. About the only thing left was her old Plymouth. This was the first night since I moved that I'd not gone to bed in Mount Olive. The first night away since I'd bought the place up yonder.

My cousin Murphy Jr. had used the room. No sign of him there, though, the paneled walls unadorned, the room tidy, as if Aunt Latrice dusted it regularly, perhaps thinking with nostalgia: What if my son hadn't gone down that deadly road, the one he traveled almost from his first night out the darkness of the womb?

Penny came back to my thoughts and I realized I hadn't called her. So I did. We talked, but I left out the bomb-making and how Johnny's corpse was left at my door with the note.

After we were done on the phone, I went back to the bedroom, the place where Murphy Jr. used to listen to rock music in the early seventies. I recalled his long blond hair, his rail-thin body, how he was tall and not encumbered yet by the weight that often overtakes Tadlocks past thirty. He'd have a cigarette in his mouth every time you'd see him from sixteen years old on, and he had a way of watching you out of the corner of his eye like he never trusted anyone, as if he didn't even trust himself. Often mothers will leave their dead children's rooms like nothing ever happened, but not this room. It was clean as a whistle and you wouldn't guess Murphy Jr. had ever been alive. He'd been dead fourteen years and there wasn't one thing in the room to say that he was ever around except for memory of him in my mind. I guess that's all that really matters.

I lay there in bed, my blue jeans still buttoned, my T-shirt off, the boots left out on the porch when I came inside. It would be easy to go to the Army recruiter and tell him I'd made a terrible mistake. Beg my way back in, at least join the reserves. It would be a lot harder to go up to Mount Olive and find Moxley and face him down, put holes in his chest with a pistol. Blowing big holes through him with a piece of iron in my hand, then live with the consequences.

For a moment I thought about going over that same bridge my cousin Murphy Jr. hit in 1975. Maybe taking down the west side on I-10 over the Mighty Mississippi, jerking the wheel hard and going over, two hundred feet down to the water. Or just causing one hell of a wreck like he did and seeing myself burn alive in a heap of destroyed cars.

I imagined what it would feel like falling down to the chemical-filled water, every possible pollutant below like molten sludge. Would the fall or the water kill me?

Nothing could be more logical to think about, to go on back up there to Mount Olive, pull open the wire gap with me and Sam Bullfinch alone, and tell him, "Something ain't right about this place. I don't want it. I'm sorry to waste your time, but I'm not interested." Let somebody else give a pound of flesh. Make the sale to some other dumb-ass. Let someone else have his hide ripped off.

Why not just roll back time like a home movie. Why not?

God doesn't let time roll back often. He wouldn't approve. I've found that God just kind of lets it all go crazy on this earth, lets the fires burn, lets the little babies cry for the milk of a dead mother's breast. God just kind of stays out of it all, lets one frame of the movie play after the other, in sequence, always forward and never in reverse. That's how this world works.

This was all nonsense—buying a house and land only to be attacked by the neighbor, a goddamned nutsoid of a neighbor, a sociopath neck-deep with the law, a badass that hadn't been trumped yet, a man with dogs that kill on command.

The room was warm, so I went over to the good working air conditioner in the window and turned it on. It buzzed and rattled but came alive shortly, the noise a comfort and a distraction from my thinking.

After a time it got cooler in the room, eleven o'clock according to the watch on my arm. I turned the lamp off beside the bed and stared at the ceiling, and wandered along in my mind about a place just as dark. Before I could visit that place very long, I was falling asleep.

CHAPTER 14

When morning broke, pink light flooded the bedroom window. I slipped on a clean T-shirt, and left on my blue jeans, the ones I had worn the day before without washing them. When I left the bedroom, I saw Uncle Red and Aunt Latrice in the kitchen smoking cigarettes, already dressed, probably on their third cup of coffee apiece.

"I called your uncles and cousins and they're going to meet us over at Carlin's place on the Tangilena River this evening. Jerry and Nolan are coming, and their boys, too. Meet us out there at five o'clock, you hear?" Uncle Red crushed a cigarette in the ashtray.

"OK," I said.

"I've got a few things to do today, some crab pots to buy in Milltown from an old boy named Mike Octave. You don't get in no trouble. Don't stray from around the house."

"I need to be looking for work. I don't have a lot of money left after buying the truck and the land, paying for the electric hook-up, gas and all. Maybe five hundred dollars in the bank total."

Aunt Latrice brought me a cup of coffee. The coffee was black and strong, hot as hell water. I tasted it and put three teaspoons of sugar in it and stirred.

"Linda Tompkins says they're hiring at Tidwell's Warehouse, the big storehouse off 190. She said her boy is making seven dollars an hour to start," said Aunt Latrice.

This was the second time I'd heard of jobs at the new warehouse, I recalled.

"Go see Seth Herman at Tidwell's if you want a job," Uncle Red said. "Unless you want to run crabs with me, fish a while. Seth knows you're back home. Told me to tell you to come see him. He needs a security guard and wants somebody with military experience."

I was almost out of money, and the fishing didn't sound so good, considering that the last time we went all we accomplished was to have Moxley vandalize the truck. The biggest thing I was looking for right then was stability, one way or the other.

Two hours later, after eating some biscuits, I put on the dress clothes that I'd brought with me and went to see Mr. Herman, a man with his necktie tied loose in a big knot, the top button on his white shirt left unfastened.

I filled out the application, and Mr. Herman said I could start work in two weeks if my references and background check went well. I'd heard this before but told him I could wait, no problem. I had no other offers.

I spent the rest of the morning bush-hogging the field behind Aunt Cat's place using Uncle Red's Massey Ferguson tractor, watching quail fly into the air at eye-level, seeing rabbits run from the machine. I'd do about anything to fill the day. I was tired of reading history books about wars and politics that I'd checked out from the Pickleyville Public Library a week back.

Penny had given me her beeper number, the beeper she carried for work, and I buzzed her once I got done with the tractor.

She called me at Aunt Cat's where I was resting on the couch. She said we could meet at the cafeteria over at the Bayou Square Mall near Ninth Ward Hospital for a late lunch.

I waited in the foyer at the restaurant, sitting there beside a blind Creole man ninety years old who talked to me about the Good Lord as if Christ was seated next to him, hand on his shoulder.

I told the old man good-bye when I saw Penny walk up in her green nurse's outfit and white overcoat, a stethoscope looping out of one pocket.

The old feller stood up. He waved his hand across his chest like a Roman Catholic. "Thy ways will be the way of sorrows, thy feet hardened unto the earth, thy neck stiff, and thy soft heel bruised by iniquity. Blessed be ye in the name of Almighty Jesus H. Christ."

I found the man's words strange. I left him where he stood, his dark eyeglasses following me as I walked away.

Penny kissed me on the cheek and we got in line. She seemed cheerful and I was trying hard not to act depressed, but she caught me. "Why the long face?"

"I'll tell you when we sit down to eat."

She crinkled a brow.

We went through the cafeteria line and got our meals and carried them on plastic trays. We found a table far enough away from the retirees eating their lunches.

"So, what's up?" she asked.

I told her all about the dog and the letter ice-picked to him.

"Oh, my God." She put a napkin over her food.

"I'm sorry about ruining your roast beef."

She stared down at the napkin covering her plate. "I'll take it back with me and put it in the staff fridge."

"Penny, do you own a gun?"

"An old sixteen-gauge shotgun at home. I don't even know if it works. It was my father's. I also have a .38 in my car. I hate how it bucks when I shoot it."

"You're joking."

"No, I bought it just in case my ex-husband ever wanted to get back together with me."

"Is it loaded?"

"Sure. What good is an unloaded gun to a helpless woman?"

I knew she was having fun at my expense. "I don't want you going up to Mount Olive to see me for any reason. It's way too dangerous."

I finished eating my lunch and we put her food in a Styrofoam box, and went out to the parking lot. I walked her to the Toyota and kissed her, promising to give her some shooting lessons.

"Jesse, I won't ever need lessons on shooting a gun. I've been shooting pistols with my brother since I was ten years old."

I laughed and told her she was probably a better shot than I was.

Later that afternoon, I drove west on Highway 190 headed to Carlin's. Past the airport, pines bordered both sides of the road, young, maybe twenty feet high, in rows like soldiers. It amazed me how much of the land had grown up in pines. I remembered as a kid seeing long stretches of hardwoods, many varieties of oak, hickory, and beech, trees that shaded country roads with a canopy like an archway. The money was in the pines and I guess money's about all that really matters nowadays.

The pines gave way to cypress on both sides of 190 as I neared the river swamp. I crossed the river near Hardin, and turned into Carlin's drive, and then doubled back down a furrowed road to his house.

Carlin lived with his second wife Nan, a woman he married not long after I went into the Army. Much was made of his divorce and taking up with this woman, how she was a bookkeeper for the Police Jury where he used to work, how he left his first wife for an ugly woman. Uncle Red often joked he'd leave Latrice only for a better looking model, and that Carlin, at best, took one step down for Nan.

Carlin's house was on seven-foot stilts overlooking an unkempt yard that flooded sometimes when the river got up with silt-water. Several pickup trucks were parked in Carlin's yard, some operable, some not. Uncle Red's Ford was visible. I didn't recognize the other vehicles.

The wooden steps up to the house were slick, as a brief shower had come earlier in the day. Green scum and mold covered the steps. It was treacherous, a wonder somebody hadn't broken their fool neck going up or down.

"Come on in and get you a cold beer," I heard Carlin holler even before I'd reached the top of the steps. He met me at the sliding glass door with an icy can of Miller Light. I took the beer and popped the top. Carlin gave me a rough shove on the arm and hugged me, and I liked to have dropped the beer on the floor.

I shook hands with Uncle Jerry and Uncle Nolan. Their sons had to bowl in a league that night and couldn't come, they said. Likewise, Carlin's two boys, John Wayne and Charles, were in Texas working on a gas pipeline.

"They's enough beer for a hundred of us. Nan's gone to the coast. Old Carlin can play a little now. You help yourself," Uncle Jerry said. By the looks of his bloodshot eyes he'd swallowed plenty of beer already, the party starting real early in the day.

The house smelled of cigar smoke, and Uncle Jerry had one lit and smoldering. A part of his lower lip, small but noticeable, was shaved off, surgically removed on account of lesions from mouth cancer. He's like everybody else; he doesn't learn from his mistakes. He puffed happily on the cigar.

"I called y'all here to tell you we got us a problem." Uncle Red spoke above the extended greetings. The glee over beer and new company died down to a minimum in a couple of seconds. All of a sudden, the men had dour looks on their faces, every one of them, kind of a Tadlock grimace passed on to every male child in the family, a kind of stoic response to the hard times my people have felt in this uninhabitable place where we have scratched out an existence for more than one hundred years. Even Carlin hadn't missed his cue, the muscles in his face turning stony, as if some messenger would come through the door and tell him that all of his children and his wife have shot one another dead in a bloody gunfight and he was alone at fifty-three. That he was the only one left to pass on the family name, and that he was infertile himself from a degenerating disease of the groin; he was the dead end, and all was lost, like in the Book of Job.

Uncle Red spoke up, "Jesse has done good for hisself, serving a twelve-year hitch in the Army. He brung hisself home to live in peace. Bought hisself a little land up in Mount Olive on the state line, just a right fine start for a young man. More than I had at his age, I tell you the God's own truth. And a no-good bastard named Cotton Moxley has cost Jesse a job at the Sheriff's Office, what he'd been promised, and has killed his mama's dog, even threatened Jesse in the yard of his own house and told him to leave, to goddamned leave his own place. He's slashed my tires, all four, and stole my truck battery while we were fishing. What do you say to that? That's why I'm here." Uncle Red was standing for his little speech. The room was silent save the faint spell cast by a radio playing Hank Williams's "The Lost Highway."

"Well, what we got to do with all that? I ain't even seen Jesse twice in ten years," said Carlin, a fake grin on his wrinkled face, the air burdened with his statement.

I knew Carlin had just said something he might later regret.

"Now Carlin, blood is blood," Uncle Jerry said, placing his beer on the table just a little harder than he ought to. "I mean going to the service is just like being right here amongst us."

"Jesse wasn't here when we buried his grandma," Carlin responded. "He wasn't here when Uncle Esco was buried. That boy ain't even dug a grave since he left for the service. He wasn't hardly down there at the hospital with his own mama when she had cancer. He ain't even buried his own mama. That's a disgrace. Damn, he's been long gone."

My ears were hot. I wanted to answer him but I held my peace.

"Carlin, he's your dead brother's son. He's blood," Uncle Nolan said, tipping back a felt fedora on his high forehead.

"I don't care. He ain't had to move all the way up to Mount Olive. He could have stayed right around here," Carlin said.

"Carlin, it ain't but thirty-five miles from here. Have you had too much liquor? Has it cooked your goddamned brain? Now, we need to take care of some business." Uncle Jerry gazed at Carlin like he was near about ready to fight.

Carlin stood up barely five-eight, but he acted like he was seven feet tall. He blew his chest up like he was the biggest man in the room. "This ain't happening. I don't even want to know about it. Don't even have a dog in the fight. If he's in trouble, let the law help him. Let him what wants to help, help. But I ain't for it."

"You said all you're going to say?" Uncle Red asked him.

"I said what's gonna be said."

"And the rest of you? Jerry, Nolan?"

There was another silence. Each man nodded. It was hard to read either of them.

"Then let's get the hell out of here. Don't need to have a pussy up in our goddamned business." Uncle Red slapped Carlin upside the head, backhanding him before he could get out the way. Carlin's neck jerked. A slap not to inflict pain but to embarrass. A slap to dare him to respond. A slap from his big brother in his own house.

"Get out. Go on. Get the devil's hell off my land. All y'all. Get the hell away from here," Carlin screamed.

The party was over. The four of us left through the glass door.

We went out into the yard. The men smoked. I took a pinch from Uncle Nolan's can of snuff, a rare occurrence for me.

"This is what I want," Uncle Red told the men gathered in the yard. "This son of a bitch Moxley is going to get his, but right now, I want us to take over the night from him. I want Jesse to go on back up to his place, but I don't want him there alone. Nolan, you and Jerry ain't working, are you?"

Each man said no. They leaned against the bed of Uncle Red's Ford.

"I got some plans and I want to keep Jesse protected, not left up yonder by hisself to be screwed with. I can stay on the weekends. I don't believe it's going to take too long before we get all this shit straightened out."

The men doled out the night watches for the coming weeks, who would stay when, starting on Saturday night. Then we all left in a convoy of trucks out of Carlin's drive.

Moxley would have more of a challenge than he might want, more than me alone. That's all that mattered to me.

In the house of darkness, though, I bet Carlin was sitting in the living room sulking, drinking probably, glass after glass of corn whiskey, teary-eyed over his older brother pushing him around, somehow deep inside questioning his own cowardice.

CHAPTER 15

O n Wednesday morning at four-thirty the alarm clock went off with a shrill buzz. I nearly fell out of bed. The night before Uncle Red asked me to set it. I immediately got ready to leave. Before Aunt Latrice was awake, well before daylight, we were headed to Mount Olive. Inside the cab of the Ford truck sat a wooden box filled with bombs. The rifles were behind the seat. The pistols were loaded and placed between us.

Uncle Red was an unpredictable, indiscernible man. He'd taken this problem of mine on and we were in it together. Maybe the death of his own son, the distance between them before Murphy Jr. died, was the cause of his commitment to my welfare. I didn't know, but together, I did know that Cotton Moxley would have to fight hard, not to mention my two other uncles now in the little war as well.

"I've done some more checking on my own," Uncle Red said. "Went to see Pete Higgman at the power company. He knows everybody. He's worked right-of-ways for them, maybe thirty years for Louisiana Power and Light, and for the paper mill in Bogalusa before that."

"What did you find out?"

"He knew Balem and his grandpa, Buck Moxley," Uncle Red went on. "We got a barrel of nuts for our troubles."

"You wouldn't mind explaining more of what you learned, would you? I already know we got troubles."

"I'm getting there, son. From what I gathered, Buck Moxley used to beat his boys and girls, grandkids too, with a bullwhip when he got mad, out in the yard so he could get some swing on his leather whip. That's what turned Balem so goddamned crazy.

"About the time the boy was thirteen years old, Pete was cutting a big right-of-way up in the north end of the parish. They bought the land at a fair price, a right-of-way across old man Moxley's land, a big power line up there, according to Pete. He had his niggers out there cutting a big stretch of timber around the border of the Moxley place, the house you bought, and Pete left his foreman, George, out there to cut the trees. Maybe six or seven in the crew, a couple of tractor men, and saw men as well.

"All of a sudden they heard shots fired and directly bark went to flying off of a tree beside a worker. Bullet lead would ping off tractor steel. Maybe six or eight sharp and accurate rounds were fired to scare, not to kill, not yet anyway.

"Pulpwood niggers got plumb shook up, Pete said. They couldn't see nobody. Just racket from the woods and tree bark a-flying. Pete recalled that the damned niggers walked out the woods a mile to the blacktop. George went and found Pete Higgman and begged him to do something or there wouldn't be no more right-of-ways cut by the crew." Uncle Red stalled the story to light a cigarette in the darkness of the cab.

"What happened?"

"Pete knew it was them crazy-assed Moxleys, the boy probably, though the girls were just as assed-up. So he drove over to your very own house, the old Moxley place, and told Buck he better do something or the power company would cut off his lights forever.

"The old man went out in the woods and found his grand-boy Balem and took the rifle and beat him with it. Broke several ribs with it, to hear Pete tell it. Never another shot was fired the whole time they was up yonder in the woods. Not a goddamned peep. They barely got all the right-of-way cut even after begging the hands back to work."

Uncle Red was quiet all of sudden like he wanted it to sink in, like he wanted me to get enough of it in my mind for it to be some kind of lesson about handling Moxley. I was listening, but unsure if I was taking what he wanted me to glean from it.

This was the first time Uncle Red had been to the place in Mount Olive. It was still dark when we pulled into the yard. The porch light was on and could be seen like a low-hung star way off from the main gravel road.

Uncle Red asked me to show him where Moxley had made threats, where Johnny was found dead, so I showed him.

He admired the board and batten wood on the porch, heart pine boards cut twelve inches wide. He complained about how folks covered the pine and cypress with asbestos siding in the fifties and sixties, ruining the beauty of the wood. However, the Moxleys had not done so and it added character to the old farmhouse.

We drank hot coffee from a stainless steel thermos bottle, the coffee burning my tongue a little bit.

A commotion sounded up the road, a clanking of steel on steel, of a diesel engine attempting to shift gears. The headlights flashed and I was alarmed, the vehicle sounding off. A truck and long trailer pulled into the grassed-over drive of mine.

Uncle Red smiled, flicking a cigarette butt into the yard, over the edge of the porch.

A one-ton truck driven by Sid Willie made the noise. Sid was a friend of ours from Edwinburg. Behind his truck on a trailer sat his bulldozer, a 450 Case. A 450 is not a large dozer but it's plenty big enough for home use. When daylight broke, I sat on the right side on the machine by Uncle Red, on the fender inside the cab. The M16 was between us, and the M1 rested on the other side of my uncle. Our extra ammo was in a canvas bag.

We made a perimeter around the place, toppling bushy tallow trees, pushing over briar thickets. By noon we started making some piles. My legs were cramped from sitting on the fender.

Then Uncle Red used a stick of homemade pipe bomb to blow out a stump near the dry creek branch. My ears rang and the ground trembled slightly. Water, muddy water, began to fill the hole as if we'd exposed the veins of a spring.

We doused the piles with dozens of gallon milk jugs full of burnt motor oil. Uncle Red acquired the oil from a gas station and brought it to Mount Olive in the bed of his truck. This went on for hours, pushing up brush piles and small trees, occasionally blowing out a stump with a pipe bomb like a stick of dynamite, lighting brush piles.

About eleven o'clock, I suppose the temptation was far too great. I saw a man riding horseback on what looked like a mammoth, perhaps a Belgian or Percheron crossed with quarter horse or thoroughbred, a dappled horse with a dark gray mane and tail that must have weighed sixteen hundred pounds. The rider had a white beard, three pit bulls trotting at his stirrup. He was loping the animal in front of my place on the gravel road near the power line.

After seeing the man and dogs, I pointed to the gravel road. Uncle Red saw him and stopped the dozer. We got off.

"Son, lean over on the dozer track and take aim at one of them dogs. Don't stop shooting till you kill one of them."

Moxley wasn't on my land yet but he was moving quickly down the road almost directly in front of the property.

I took hold of the M16 and changed the selector lever off of full-auto. I rushed to take aim without thinking. Our work removing trees that morning made it a straight shot. I knew exactly why Uncle Red was clearing the land now: to keep Moxley from sneaking up on us. I knew he wasn't doing this just to lay claim on the land, or to piss Moxley off, though this probably ran through his mind.

I'd made shots like this before in the military, but not since boot camp in Georgia. The weapon was tight on my cheek, and I bore down on it, leaned against the blade of the dozer, bracing the rifle against the steel. But I couldn't pull the trigger. I stalled. Damn, I seized up, unable to take the shot.

From behind I heard, "To hell, son," and then an explosion. *Pah-Yow. Pah-Yow.* Two shots behind me. Uncle Red shot the .30-06.

Moxley went out of sight momentarily. I jumped, banging the M16 against the iron. It was a damn miracle the weapon didn't discharge.

I then saw Moxley running the horse in the opposite direction, a yellow bulldog beside him. Only one dog followed the galloping draft horse.

In retreat now, you sumbitch. In retreat now, I thought.

When I looked back to Uncle Red, he was sighting in Moxley at two hundred yards away, calculating his next move, his finger on the trigger, the muscles in his right hand starting to tighten. Then he released, turning the trigger loose. He stared at me.

"Next time I tell you to fire that weapon, you had better damn well pull the trigger. You hear?"

"Yes sir, I hear."

Uncle Red and I were careful the rest of the day; he was driving the dozer and I sat up on the side of the cab. I was watching the distance for Moxley, knowing he would seek revenge.

After the day's work, when it got near dark, we walked to the ridge at the gravel road where the two dogs had been killed. I guess they were shot on public land. I don't know. The dogs were ten yards from my property line, and I suppose it was a benefit to the public at large regardless, killing the damned pit bulls, though shooting anything on a parish road was surely illegal.

Even at the distance, the .30-06 made tremendous holes in the dogs' flesh, entering like a finger, exiting like a fist. The tongue of the first dog, a black and white bulldog, was curled out the side of his mouth, blue and swollen. The other, a red-nosed auburn-colored dog, was shot through the side of the neck, the bullet taking off his left ear in a circle of exploded skin. Each dog was stiff as I kicked him. Stiff as dead dogs. Dead as doornails, just as dead as Johnny, I thought. I laughed.

I was surprised by the laughter coming from my lips, unsure of what brought it on. It was kind of senseless in such a way that only laughter could help us bear it.

Back in the pasture, we lit the remaining piles of briars, scrub tallow trees. From the looks of the place, it was all farmland maybe seven or eight years ago, but it was taken over by wild things.

We'd done good work and now the diesel and burnt motor oil was doing its part, too, causing fire to engulf the drought-ridden greenery.

Six piles burned. I could now see all around the property with the scrub trees out of the way. It would be far harder to sneak up on the house during the day, and far harder to hide during the night, and I knew it would make a difference when we took over the place for good.

At about five-thirty my skin was almost numb from the ride on the dozer, the vibration troubling my bones. The image of those dogs kept after me, the way they smiled dead grins. I knew this was an affront to Moxley and he would come back, and I also questioned how close Uncle Red was to putting a bullet into Moxley himself, and whether this piece of ground was worth the risk. How much is it worth? I asked myself. Is it worth dying for? Is it worth life in the penitentiary? Is it worth the chair at Angola?

I couldn't answer this. And in not answering it, I did answer. I was frozen like one of the bulldogs in a trajectory, unable to change directions. I guessed it wouldn't stop till gravity took its natural course of things.

We left that evening as soon as Sid returned to pick up his dozer. The bulldozer had been used for a full day's work. Uncle Red paid the man, and I could see that it cost two hundred-fifty dollars, cash, a small cost for what security might bring. We loaded up and went back to Uncle Red's house and I took with me some clean clothes, a bag of clothes to get by on till I returned.

When we got to Packwood Corners, Aunt Latrice said Carlin called for me. This seemed odd, almost as if she'd gotten things confused, so I called him back. He was weepy on the phone, the sound in his voice like he'd been drinking all day. I knew he was flat-assed drunk.

"I'm going to fix everything, Jesse. I've got a way to fix it all."

"Uh-huh. How are you going to fix it?" I asked.

"Do you remember how Red called me a pussy last night?"

I delayed, didn't want to say anything to a drunk man.

"Do you remember?"

"I do."

"Well, I tell you what I did. I got me a way to your man Moxley and he ain't gonna be a-bothering you no more, not after tonight."

"No?" I asked, questioning.

"Naw, son. He ain't gonna be a-bothering you no more." He said good-bye and hung up.

This gave me plenty of cause to speculate. I relayed the conversation to Uncle Red after he got out of the shower, dressed in a white T-shirt and a pair of blue jeans, the shoulders on him bunched with muscle even at his age.

"Goddamn he's crazy. I can't stand for him to be around me with all that bullshit. He ain't never right in the head no more, and don't pay jack shit attention to him," Uncle Red said.

CHAPTER 16

Uncle Jerry called later that evening. He said that Carlin had been badly hurt and was headed to Ninth Ward Hospital in Pickleyville. That's about all we knew.

Uncle Red's truck whistled down the interstate like it was propelled by jet fuel, and in fifteen minutes we arrived at the emergency room. The place was swarming with family, Aunt Nan sobbing. Three deputies were there already. Big Cajun Ambulance Service brought Carlin to the ER. It was unexplainable how Carlin stayed alive. The paramedics were wheeling him into the ER strapped to a gurney. When I got close enough to see his head, it appeared wrapped in gauze bandages like a mummy. They said his face was repeatedly jabbed with an ice pick.

Two things encouraged me about the situation right off, though. First, I saw Penny. She was on her shift. I knew she wouldn't bullshit me about his condition. We were there six hours, a bunch of Tadlocks and Nan's people. Carlin's ex-wife, my former aunt, even showed up to check on him.

The second thing that encouraged me was the paramedics saying it looked far worse than it really was. Paramedics are almost never optimistic.

The morning wore me down to a nub as I sat in the hospital waiting room. Carlin was going to be OK. Indeed, his looks declared the worst of the incident. The doctor was able to stop the bleeding quickly, and no arteries were punctured. He went from the emergency room to the intensive care unit without much trouble, no surgery needed.

When the doctor was done with Carlin and he was able to talk a little, we were given a special dispensation to see him by Penny. He confessed to us that he knew Moxley from way back. He'd bought a pit bull bitch from him once and had dealt with Moxley for the express purpose of buying tools, mostly stolen tools he used for carpentry work. Moxley stole day and night, and as water finds its own level, so do the things of others find buyers when stolen—someone owns, another steals, and yet another profits through buying what he wants at a discount. The buyer also gets a real charge out of having cheap what another paid full price for, perhaps with interest.

According to what Carlin told to us, he had arranged to buy an air compressor from Moxley, and they were to meet a few miles north of Hardin at the Rebel Cock Pit and Café, a popular hangout for dog fighters and other human refuse who liked to gamble on the fights. In Louisiana, it's illegal to fight animals, but the state legislators decided chickens weren't animals and therefore it was perfectly lawful to fight a bird to the death. Dogfighting was illegal, but it fit together with cockfighting like dove hunting and baited fields. Dogfighting was just kept quiet.

Carlin said he paid cash money for the air compressor, making the exchange out in the gravel parking lot at the Rebel. The lot was near empty by this time, only a couple of vehicles left. Moxley helped Carlin load the equipment into the back of his Toyota truck.

Then he told Moxley his own nephew was his new neighbor up in Mount Olive, and that he would sure appreciate it if Moxley's cut the boy some slack.

Moxley cut him some slack, all right. From his back pocket—

without any warning—he pulled an ice pick and began plunging it into Carlin's shoulder and chest, his face. The size differential between the two men, about a hundred pounds of muscle, and the element of surprise made it impossible to ward off the attack. By the time a teenaged boy named Greg, a waiter at the short-order café inside the chicken fights, came upon Carlin's bloody body, Moxley was long gone. Greg called an ambulance, and Carlin was coming in and out of consciousness from blood loss, in shock by the time he got to the hospital.

I had mixed feelings. He tried to help me, but Carlin was a man of Baxter Parish, and he packed all the history of one. My uncle could not be trusted, something almost innate with him, and an ice pick to the chest and shoulders and neck and face was the way things come around for those who can't keep their alliances in order.

This made the questions bigger for me, and I suppose bigger for Uncle Red as well. First, Carlin wanted a deal. He knew Moxley and the bargain on the equipment was too hard to pass up. He could have let us know he had business with my adversary, that Moxley was old so and so to him, and that he wanted no involvement because of business, after all, business was thicker than blood. But what complicated things was Carlin trying to mix business and blood. I would have liked to respect him for trying to make my way a little easier, but I didn't know if I could. I couldn't feel very sorry for his plight.

As far as Uncle Red was concerned, I think he felt pity for his younger brother, pity that I've never witnessed before with him. I have known Uncle Red my whole life and I don't believe I've ever seen him express sorrow for either things he has done nor things others have done to him. Uncle Red doesn't suffer fools gladly, and the hard staring he did at Carlin told enough. In his eyes was a deep sorrow, and I do think he wished he'd not involved Carlin with my land troubles in the first place, as if he should have known better.

About five o'clock in the morning we were ready to leave Ninth Ward Hospital to go back home to get provisions for another day's work in Mount Olive. Carlin had stabilized, and he looked like he might make it home within a week or so.

On the way out the door we had a conversation with Uncle Red's brothers, Uncle Nolan and Uncle Jerry. Each of them said they'd talked to their wives and they couldn't have any part in my defense. The stabbing of Carlin was proof they didn't belong in this fight. They said I had been gone too long, that I hadn't taken part in family business, that I favored my mama's people, the Nards, far more than the Tadlocks.

Outside the emergency room on the sidewalk, Uncle Red pointed to me. "Take a look, Jerry, Nolan. Do you see a pissant Nard there, or goddamned Tadlock?"

I stood, watching Uncle Jerry and Uncle Nolan as they walked away, down the sidewalk to the door, back into the I.C.U. waiting area, never answering the question.

CHAPTER 17

Uncle Red and I ate breakfast at the Waffle Hut near I-55. Not a word was said about Carlin or my other uncles. We ate in silence till halfway through my waffle, when I asked Uncle Red something that was bothering me. "Where's all of this going?

"Us and Moxley?"

"Right."

"Either kill him or let him kill us. No middle ground."

Nothing else was said the whole meal. I finished my waffle and Uncle Red finished his eggs, grits, and toast and we left.

It seemed extreme, but I just didn't know how to handle it. I didn't know a good way out.

When we arrived at Mount Olive daylight was just breaking. The piles of brush and stumps were still hot and smoldering, gray smoke at tree-level on the horizon, deadwood from rotten trees still on fire as coals glowed in the piles.

We were cautious, not sure that Moxley wasn't there hiding in the house, waiting with a gun. Carlin refused to identify his assailant to the law, so the chances of involving the authorities were slim, not that they would have been willing to get involved anyhow. Perhaps his wife might talk him into telling the truth, if Nan could draw out the courage in her husband somehow.

You could see for several hundred yards in all directions. I started to think this had been an ingenious move, making a clearing out of the place.

Looked at from the truck, the house didn't seem to be tampered with. I was relieved the house was still there. I figured the farmhouse might be down to ashes when I returned. I smelled a strong odor as I pulled into the yard about a half a minute before my uncle. It smelled like a polecat, a skunk, and I figured maybe one had been there sometime in the night, run out of his dwelling by all the dozer work and the fires.

The revolver was beside me and the M16 was behind the seat. I parked under the carport.

Uncle Red drove his truck around behind mine, the cab pointed in the direction of the highway.

"You smell skunk?" I asked as I met Uncle Red at his truck door. We both walked toward the front porch.

He sniffed the air. "Kind of heavy."

We climbed the steps to the porch, the pistols jammed in our waists like outlaws. The closer I got to the porch, the stronger the stench. Something wasn't right.

I heard a rumbling noise inside the house that sounded like growling. I motioned to Uncle Red and we stood at the door quietly, holding our breath to hear, listening to the sounds of growling inside the house, the scent of a skunk keen in our nostrils. Perhaps the skunk is under the house, I thought, but what about the growling? Skunks don't growl. Hell, I know that much about skunks.

"Something's in the house," Uncle Red said, as he motioned for me to get off the porch.

Back at the truck, I took out the M16. I returned to the front door. Uncle Red took the side door at the screen porch.

When I eased the door open, the smell hit me in the mouth like a club. I gagged. At one end of the hall stood a half-dead-looking coyote the size of a German shepherd, its back arched, ears up.

I didn't want the coyote to run off, much less whatever other animal was trapped inside. I slammed the door shut. The phone still wasn't working, so I drove back to the country grocery and called the Sheriff's Office, telling them that I'd been burglarized, and giving them the address.

While I was gone, Uncle Red had two more piles burning again with motor oil, and the fire reached the low limbs on the pines nearby, twenty-foot flames.

We stowed the guns behind the truck seat and waited for the sheriff's deputy to show up.

"You reckon the skunk's still alive?" I asked Uncle Red.

"No. From the smell and the coyote, it's probably dead."

My face was hot with anger. A part of me wanted to go over to Moxley's house and throw a pipe bomb into the front room, kill whatever or whoever was there, his wife and kid if I had to. My mind went back to Carlin in the hospital, his face cut up like he'd kissed a rabid porcupine. But I did know a woman and kid were involved with Moxley, and I didn't want to hurt them or spend a lifetime behind bars, or worse.

Deputy McLin pulled up the drive and into the yard, the same narrow-faced man from before. He was taking his time getting out of his car, trying to see what to make of the situation, I suppose.

"Well, glad to see you're still enjoying life in God's country," the deputy said. He had a crooked smile on his face, a smirk.

"Sure. Plenty of the Good Lord's disciples around here to make life a pleasure," Uncle Red replied.

"You wouldn't have a permit to burn those piles, would you?" the deputy asked.

I could tell my uncle was filled with the spirit. He was blowing smoke from a Camel through his nostrils. "Yes sir. I reckon we do. It's called a damned deed to this land, a damned clear deed. Since when do you care to enforce the law anyway?"

The deputy looked at Uncle Red, and then he looked at me. "What can I help you with?"

My uncle pointed at the deputy sheriff. "A son of a bitch named Moxley broke in and has put a coyote and a skunk in the house. I want you to see it."

"Are they inside now?" asked the deputy.

"Yes sir," I said.

The three of us stood on the porch a moment, then I opened the front door and stepped back. The smell flooded the front of the house, the rankest stench I have ever smelled.

Directly the coyote ran out of the front door full throttle, out into the yard, never looking back, his haunches moving like he'd been lit with a flame. The deputy drew his pistol and put a handkerchief over his face.

We walked in behind him. The center hallway was full of vomit, puke from the animals. The skunk had sprayed the house from one end to the other, all four rooms, the two bedrooms, and the kitchen. Splotches of blood traced the walls as if sprayed by a garden sprinkler, and skunk piss was all over, skunk guts on the couches.

Two skunks: One skunk lay dead in the living room where my mama's furniture was undoubtedly ruined. Another skunk lay dead underneath my bed, and it appeared that the skunk ran beneath the bed trying to flee. Blood was all over the room, shit and blood. My eyes were watering.

The deputy inspected the locks on the doors with the handkerchief over his mouth and it seemed that whoever entered did so by picking the locks, no sign of forced entry. He must have come through the front door, as the side door had a hook latch on the inside undisturbed.

"So you say you believe Cotton did this?"

"Hell yeah. He raises skunks and coyotes, all kinds of animals," I told him.

"OK. I'll try to go see him. I'll try to talk to him. Ask what he was doing last night."

"Ask him how it felt ice-picking my brother while you're at it," Uncle Red said.

"Whatever you say, chief. In the meantime, perhaps you ought to get yourself a good guard dog."

"I had one and Moxley killed it," I told the deputy.

The deputy left the porch.

After disposing of the animals, the two skunks, we spent the rest of the morning loading much of the furniture into the smoldering piles near the house, piles we'd pushed with the dozer. In the clearing, upon burning piles of brush, the furniture my mother had spent a lifetime collecting, was on fire. I knew redeeming the pieces of cloth-covered wood was a lost cause. We burned the mattresses and the couches, the soft chairs, anything penetrable by skunk spray. In fifty-one years of life, these possessions were about all she had gathered, and the fire destroyed it in minutes.

A little before noon, Aunt Latrice and Aunt Cat came up to the place, and they brought with them Pine-Sol, gallons of tomato juice, bleach, buckets, and mops. They started cleaning and scrubbing the floors and walls, removing the piss and blood and guts left from the night battle between feral animals in my house, the battle for life and death between a coyote and two frightened skunks.

The phone man finally arrived that afternoon and turned on service. He looked at me like I was some kind of alien. "Y'all plan to live here?" he asked, incredulous over the smell. "This is the damnedest skunk scent I reckon I ever sniffed."

Nobody acknowledged his comment. He got me to sign an order saying the phone was working up to expectations. At least now I had a telephone at the place. The first person I called was my cousin Ellis Brady down in Ruthberry, at his house, it being Saturday.

Ellis said the judge had issued the restraining order and they would try to serve Moxley, that he was not to be within a hundred feet of me, assuming they could ever find him to serve the papers. If this were violated, the sheriff would have little choice but to arrest him and bring him before the district attorney in Ruthberry. Judge Marshall wouldn't be lenient. My cousin said this might turn the tide, put Moxley on notice that the jig was up. I told him about Carlin's accident, and I heard dead quiet on the other end of the line, a prolonged silence that bothered me.

A few seconds later Ellis reminded me of something. "Do what you have to do, but remember what I told you about Turnish Wincher?"

"How could I forget? If Moxley shows up at my place, can I shoot him?"

"Legally, only if he makes a credible threat to your person. He doesn't have to come through the door of the house, now, under the circumstances. He has to be a bona fide threat; say, he has a piece of lightered knot in his hand and is waving it. You got my drift here? Just a threat, real or perceived, but something even a dumb-ass deputy could ascertain as a threat, something any local law enforcement officer would see as plenty of reason to shoot his ass off. He'd better be armed, Jesse. Armed with something!"

"You mean stick a piece of stovewood near the body?" I asked, shifting the phone to my right ear.

"You ever considered being a lawyer?"

"No. I'm too honest."

"Well, there might be hope for you yet. Any hoot, I'll send letters to the salesman and to the bank Monday. I'll let them know you want your money back. I'll have copies of the letters if you ever need them. Let them see in writing that there is a problem. The bank might be able to clear this up if they want to. I'll give them two weeks to reply, say we'll sue the hell out of them if it doesn't come to an amicable resolution. You want your money back, right?"

"No, I don't want my money back. I'd rather have the land I paid for without harassment."

"Have it however you want."

"What will the bank do?"

"They'll either begin making some sort of conciliatory gesture, or they'll blow us off. It's always hard to tell what'll happen. We might even name Moxley in the suit with them, let the judge decipher who's at fault in this mess."

"Yeah. But will I get my land and house back without any bull-shit?"

"Who knows? If you ever need to see me, come by the office. It's summer and it's kind of slow."

"You bet."

"Try coming after daylight next time. How about it?"

"Sure. What time?"

"Try ten o'clock. I like sleeping late."

"OK."

"And one more thing."

"Uh-huh."

"Don't spend too much time in Mount Olive. Go home to Packwood Corners for a while. Lay up with that girlfriend of yours in Pickleyville and get your knob shined. Be careful. Your Uncle Red is crazy as a shit-

house rat and he might end up making you an accessory to murder."
Ellis hung up without saying good-bye, just let his words roll off of his
tongue, kind of slow, and then he was gone from the line.

CHAPTER 18

There was little furniture in the house untouched by skunk scent and coyote vomit and blood. Items stowed in a cabinet or a closet were mostly all right, but even some of the clothes in the cedar robe smelled of skunk and needed washing in tomato juice and Pine-Sol. The flour in the pantry smelled of skunk. The towels in the bathroom smelled of skunk and had to be washed. What disturbed me most was how Moxley went through the locks so easily. He did it without making the slightest scuff on the doorjamb, as if he'd found a spare key on the porch and walked right in. But there wasn't a spare key.

The women were with me, Uncle Red, too, with no real hope of other reinforcements, save Penny, and I'd asked her not to come to Mount Olive. Our eyes were burning from the skunk. We couldn't take much more. The waste of it all. Finally, we decided to have a break from the mess, go home. We'd done plenty of cleaning. There wasn't any reason to lock the doors this time. I left them open with the screen door shut to allow the house to air out. Leaving Mount Olive in one piece seemed victory enough.

So, we left and went on down to Packwood Corners. It was the end of a long day. Aunt Cat and Uncle Red and Aunt Latrice convoyed to the south end with me. We flew no white flag of surrender. We were just dog-tired and worn slap out, ready to regroup.

*

After supper, about seven o'clock, Uncle Red and I went to see Carlin at Ninth Ward Hospital. It was amazing that he'd gotten better so fast, that he made it through all of the blood loss and was doing all right. When we went into his hospital room he was laughing, white gauze still around the spots where the ice pick hit his body. He was watching cable TV, he told me, and asked out loud whether they'd ever get cable in Hardin. He doubted it.

Uncle Red told him what happened with the house and the animals, how we'd burned most of the furniture. Carlin just shut his eyes tight like he was fighting back tears or anticipating some sort of slap in the face. Then he opened his eyes fast, blinking like the village idiot.

"Kill the dirty sumbitch. Awh, goddamn," he said, spit flying from his lips. "Shoot the bastard's head off. You can't play with a sumbitch. See me? I played with a no-good sumbitch. Kill the sumbitch."

His words stuck like sharp leather lashes on my back.

Uncle Red looked at his younger brother. I believe he was weighing his words. "How do you do it, Carlin?" he asked.

When we began talking to Carlin, his heart rate was ninety beats per minute. His monitor was now showing a rapid rate, one-thirty. This was bad and the conversation needed to end.

"You keep him from striking you first. Send all manner of fire down upon him. You put a boot heel on his neck. You cut off his head." The monitor hit one-forty, and a buzzer began to squeal, and a nurse entered into the room and told us to leave, and so we left.

I walked out to the ER lobby with Uncle Red. I knew Penny was off work at six o'clock.

Uncle Red took the closest door to get a smoke, and I checked at the desk to see if Penny was there a few minutes early. I went outside and found her smoking a cigarette, which surprised me. She was sitting on a concrete bench in her scrubs. Beside her sat a bald-headed nurse who was obviously queer from the way he held a cigarette and kept his left hand on his hip, elbow cocked out. Before I could greet Penny, he got up, told me to have a seat.

"Terry, that's my man, Jesse," she said.

"I'll let you two have some time," he said, and left.

She crushed her cigarette on the side of the bench and tossed it into a big aluminum ashtray.

I sat beside her, drained.

"When did you start smoking?" I asked.

"I only smoke at work."

"It killed Mama."

"Yes, and other things will kill you. I also smoke a cigarette after sex."

That surprised me too. "Yeah," I said.

She smiled. "And that means I only smoke at work."

I almost laughed. It was a nice joke. "How's Carlin doing, in your opinion?"

"Mr. Carlin'll be home in a few days. I checked this morning."

"That's good. Thanks for doing that." I told her about the coyote and the skunks and the deputy's lack of interest.

"Oh, Jesse, some of my girlfriends might have some extra furniture."

"That'd be helpful," I said.

"Why don't you come by the house tonight? I have a half-shift today. I'll cook. How's seven o'clock?"

"That's fine."

She stood, hugged and kissed me, and we said good-bye.

For many weeks after I left Baxter Parish for the Army years ago I thought about home. The distance felt good. But during the last months of my time in the service, while Mama was ill, the longing for home grew more unbearable than in the decade before.

I thought more of Penny, and how reuniting with her was unexpected, like the only good gift I had left in coming home. It was not as if home had a better appeal than many other places. There weren't many jobs; the rivers were polluted with cow shit from the dairies and hazardous waste from dumps. Not to mention the violence. Poor blacks and whites stretched from one end of the parish to the other in quarters no better than some of the worst slums in South Africa. Blacks hated the whites. Whites hated the blacks. The Sicilians in Liberty City hated both of them. The Mob ran Pickleyville, taking orders from New Orleans bosses. The south end flooded, the north end was a pine barren of illiteracy and inbreeding. The schools in the parish were among the worst in the state, and overall Louisiana's schools rank the lowest in the nation, even below Mississippi. More teenaged girls got knocked up in the parish than in Managua, Nicaragua, a recent newspaper report claimed. Taxes were high, nine cents on a dollar for all sales in town, including food. The politicians in Baton Rouge said the junior college shouldn't be more than a vo-tech, a trade school for high school dropouts, and they've tried hard to downgrade its status more than once.

My cousin Ellis used to tell me every time I came home from the service, "You're smart, Jesse T., staying away. It's a wasteland down here, and I see the worst human refuse in my law practice, on both sides of the bench. You know why Baxter Parish is long and skinny?"

I'd always say, "No."

"'Cause it's the biggest dick in Louisiana, one nut is Lake Tickfaw, the other nut is Lake Pontchartrain. Baxter Parish has been boinking Pike County up the ass for a hundred years, grabbing Amite County in one hand and Walthall County in the other. Just boinking the dogshit out of Mississippi since around the last days of the Civil War."

I'd laugh like it was the first time I'd ever heard him say it.

But at least Baxter Parish had the possibility of being home, even if it was a piss-poor home, and I'd always wanted to claim just a little piece of it for myself.

CHAPTER 19

Carlin's words circled before me, the words of my uncle who was suffering in the hospital for mixing his loyalties. I suppose he got a clear look at himself lying there in the bed, his face and upper torso like a pincushion.

The fact he wasn't talking to the law didn't surprise me, but there was something else that was intriguing, too, what Grandpa Nard, Mama's daddy, told me when I was a kid. Grandpa always said not to back a coward into a corner: he'll come out swinging, and he'll take you down in the fury of his own fear. I wondered if Carlin would lie there and never avenge himself.

Come on now, Carlin, I thought. Why stay a coward? As soon as the words passed through my mind I asked myself if I would avenge. Was I more the coward than Carlin, and what would I do if backed into a corner?

If Carlin went to the district attorney, Moxley might go down hard. He'd be one step over the line and away from whatever mojo he had on Haltom Roberts. It might save us all, but Carlin had his own trouble for buying stolen goods, perhaps decades of buying hot tools to run his house-building business on the cheap.

Talking to the D.A. would make sense in a way. But I've learned that people don't often make a lot of sense. Not as I can tell, anyway.

After riding back to Uncle Red's house and taking a bath and changing into some clean clothes, I drove down Old Sawmill Road to Pickleyville, parking the truck in front of Penny's house. Her Toyota was under the barn-looking garage out back. Floodlights illuminated the otherwise dark yard.

It was Saturday night and I figured we'd go see a movie, the movie that we missed, and go eat a good dinner. While I was away in the Army, there was a big Chinese restaurant built over on Highway 51 where I enjoyed eating whenever I came home. Folks said the goldfish in the outdoor pools weighed five pounds, and they'd get as big as sea grouper if released in Lake Tickfaw. I remembered Penny saying she planned to cook and the idea of the restaurant faded.

When I walked down the concrete path to her porch, I could hear music inside, noticeably loud. I heard the Eagles singing, "Take It Easy."

I knew she couldn't want to see me anymore than I wanted to see her. She called out for me to open the front door when I stepped onto the porch. I opened the door, walked into the living room, then the kitchen. The song ended and another started, "Let's Get It On," by Marvin Gaye.

I could see that her legs were lean and tan beneath her skirt, and I walked over to where she stood in the kitchen tossing lettuce for a salad and kissed her on the neck without warning. She tensed her shoulders. I put my hands on her waist and turned her around and I tasted the wine on her lips.

She suggested I pour myself a glass, the large gallon bottle open and half-empty on her wood table, and I did as she said. She was on her third glass and was feeling it, Marvin Gaye causing her to dance, sway. Penny moved to the music and pushed her hips into mine, and sang to the slow song, the music loud enough to feel slight vibrations on the oak floor.

After the little dance, the salad tossed, she brought out broiled chicken from her oven and string beans with bacon. We sat down at the table and began to eat, listening to the stereo play a series of tunes: Eric Clapton and Rod Stewart. Then there were more glasses of red wine for both of us.

Her cooking was good and I was impressed. The wine loosened me up and I thought about how nice it would be if the problems in Mount Olive could disappear.

"Why do you think that guy is so hell-bent? I mean, is it just the land, or something else?" she asked.

"I don't know. Maybe it's just the place and me living in it. People get killed over property lines all the time."

Her face was turning red. "Why do you have to talk like that? Y'all are the most pessimistic people in the world." She bit her upper lip.

"Penny, some people are just hard-asses. Crazy-asses. They don't make a lot of sense. I just don't know how all of this could have been prevented or how to stop it now."

"Is Ellis doing anything?"

"A restraining order."

"It won't matter, will it?"

"No, it won't stop anything from happening, but it could get Moxley thrown in jail. Maybe force the cops to do something eventually. The law can't prevent crime, it can only dole out who gets punished. Hey, you scared me by not having the front door locked," I said.

She didn't respond. She got up from the table and took our empty plates to the stainless steel sink.

I drank from a crystal glass, the wine warm in my mouth. It was a pretty glass, and I wondered if it was a wedding present from her first marriage.

We went into the living room with the wine and sat on her couch.

She put another cassette on to play and I listened to Van Morrison on the stereo. I liked her taste in music. Two lamps cast shadows in the room.

"Was it all worth it?" she asked.

"What?"

Penny was full of wine and she had a glow of sweat on her brow. "Coming home, leaving the Army. Was it all worth it? Would you do it again?"

"I'd like to tell you it was, but nothing seems completely logical right now. It's nothing like I expected. I thought I'd have a job, buy a house and live a regular life. Maybe have you too. Now everything is turned upside down. At the bottom of it all I wanted Baxter Parish to be like the Army, regimented, predictable."

"It's not, is it?"

"No. But it's good to have you again. I never had that in the Army. That's about the only part of my plans to work out so far."

She put her glass on the end table as she moved over by me and rubbed my chest with her left hand, and within a few minutes we were undressing in her queen-sized bed, on top of the covers, no longer talking, lying on our sides caressing each others' skin, kissing, holding each other.

We were not completely undressed yet, though my shirt was open, and Penny was rubbing my bare chest. I'd already unbuttoned her blouse, loosened her bra. I felt the warmth of her breasts; the pink nipples charged with a current almost like electricity when I felt them with my fingertips. I tasted her breast for the first time, the first time in over a decade. She closed her eyes.

After a moment she unbuttoned my jeans with a slight struggle. We were soon naked in the bed and massaging each other, feeling what we'd missed over the years.

I slipped myself into her thighs and she moved into me, both of us lying on our sides, facing each other. "Make love to me again, Jesse," she said.

I eased myself over her legs. I was as excited and fearful as the first time I'd made love to her more than a dozen years ago, when I was seventeen and our bed was the seat of my truck on the deserted logging road near Grandpa Nard's old place.

She squeezed and rocked beneath me and gathered me into her hand, into her softness, her thighs around me. I made love to her again, the completion of many years of running away.

After the passage of time, of lovemaking, she smoked a cigarette in bed, just one. We talked for an hour about what was actually right in the world. I did not leave her bed that night. I called Aunt Cat, who in turn called Aunt Latrice, to tell her not to expect me till morning, that I was with a buddy and all was well. No questions asked.

Penny and her bed smelled of lilacs and this was the first full night I had ever really slept with a woman, counting her, and I couldn't have been happier to end the day like this.

CHAPTER 20

I spent Sunday with Penny, in her bed and in her life, loving the warmth of her touch. She had to go back to work at six in the morning on Monday, and after she left I drove over to the junior college to exercise. My problems in Mount Olive seemed washed away, distant. Jogging was something I did religiously while in the Army, but it had been weeks since I exercised at all, and I needed to blow off some steam and sort through my plans, especially how Penny was going to change things.

The little college had a concrete sidewalk around its perimeter, and a brick football stadium Uncle Red helped build sometime before the Korean War. I went there figuring I would jog four or five miles, maybe, and run the steps. The junior college no longer played football. The old stadium would have been destroyed if it wasn't for the local high schools using it. I played two district football championships there in 1975 and '76.

I was never a graceful runner, six foot and two hundred pounds. I learned to like it, and I learned to take running at my own pace. These were hard-won miles, even when I was in boot camp and weighed less than one-eighty by the end. First I thought about the revolver, it sitting on the seat under a rag. I almost picked it up but realized quickly how impossible, and obviously illegal, jogging with a .38 would be. I looked around and saw no one for blocks. After all, it was a public place and should be patrolled regularly.

I parked under a sycamore tree at the south end of the campus on Dakota Street. I stretched my legs against the truck bumper, walked a few hundred yards and started to jog slowly, barely picking up my feet. The south Louisiana earth was still cool.

I could feel a little blood in my mouth, or perhaps it was just the new air filling my lungs when I started making a brisk stride.

Call it good fortune, but I made the circle around the campus, two miles, in fifteen minutes, not a bad time for somebody my size. I'd counted twelve squirrels along the way, more gray squirrels in view than people or cars at this time in the morning.

I passed my Chevy truck again at seven. I looked at my watch. I passed the Methodist chapel. Shortly afterward, I began to hear a rumble in the distance behind me, a loud noise like thunder. It was a metallic thunder, as unnatural to the place as the sound of a low-flying jet airplane.

It was behind me, rumbling and screaming, approaching quickly like a car. I turned around and saw a silver motorcycle one hundred feet behind me on the sidewalk. The rider's white beard swept back in the wind around his face. I froze, watching Moxley bearing down on his handlebars.

Thank God I had the presence of mind to turn around and run into a parking lot, not directly away from him, but running at an angle as fast as I could sprint toward the center of campus. The motorcycle had to slow down to jump the curb. It was following me, gaining. I made it to the edge of a two-story building, almost being clipped by a green Buick car trying to park. Then I saw that the big cycle had stainless steel hatchets poked out on both sides of the front forks like long, jagged foot pegs. I saw a human skull painted black where the headlight was supposed to be, something green stuck in the skull's mouth cavity.

Moxley waved at me when I opened the glass door to enter the building, safe. At once the rumbling took off again as quickly as it traced my path, the opposite way this time. I was just trying to get air back into my lungs as the sound began to wane.

CHAPTER 21

I went sweating and huffing and puffing into an office, and a secretary called campus security; then I called my cousin Ellis. Ellis said he would talk to the judge's clerk as soon as chambers opened and he said to tell every policeman I saw about the restraining order.

A few minutes later I learned that Moxley made a big foul-up. Before he got to the interstate, the city police in Pickleyville pulled him over. Or, rather, his rattletrap motorcycle broke down on Jimmie Davis Boulevard near I-55. It was conked-out on the shoulder of the road. The hatchets and the skull were reason enough to detain him.

A campus policeman overheard the call on the radio and let them know that the man needed to be questioned for some business on campus. By this time I was sitting in the campus security office in the walls of the stadium, trying to dry off with a towel they gave me. I couldn't believe my ears when the captain came into the room and told me that a man fitting the description I'd given to them was stopped near the interstate, no insurance, no registration, no inspection sticker, no driver's license. He had weapons on his motorbike, a .44 magnum pistol. Questions arose regarding the restraining order and my complaint, but this came out only after the initial confrontation between Moxley and the police. The arrest was made, according to the captain, too, for impersonating an officer. Moxley carried a Baxter Parish Sheriff's Office badge attached to his wallet. He was arrested and being booked in downtown Pickleyville for a half-dozen charges unrelated to me. By nine o'clock he was behind bars. I drove to the city police station to identify the man who tried to run me over.

Inside the police headquarters was a long hallway, and at the end of it a gray steel door. A tall officer named Gigliardo opened the door for me after taking my statement. I saw a window in a room, one-way glass, the officer told me, and five men were brought into the room. They were in a lineup and couldn't see out, I was assured.

The men were a ramble of misfits, two in orange jump-suits that said TRUSTY in bold black letters across the front, and one man with a missing left eye and a torn flannel shirt, and another man in a gray leisure suit. I suppose they just emptied the halls to form the lineup. Moxley stood defiant-looking, his face sunk in his thick white beard, the skin around his nose and eyes covered in a sprinkle of scars. Moxley stood in line, dressed in a yellow western shirt with the sleeves cut off at the shoulder, blue jeans, and dirty cowboy boots. He was the most muscular man there, by far the tallest and stoutest, and by the way he twitched and clenched his body, I figured some truth might be in the tales of his drug abuse. Moxley wore a gold rodeo belt buckle, and it had a black skull in the dead center of the steel. Old Moxley had a way of looking at the glass, a kind of ugly superior look that made me know he thought he was above the law.

I told Gigliardo and another officer named Simmons that the man at the far left, holding a Number 5 poster board in his hands, was indeed the one who tried to run me over. I gave them his name and I reiterated the business of the restraining order issued by Judge Marshall. The officers thanked me and said I could leave; they would take care of all of this business from here on out. They advised me to go on about my day. I would be called for an arraignment, and Moxley would be booked on the additional charges.

I went to the pay phone and called Aunt Latrice, all but dancing in celebration in the long hallway at the Pickleyville police station. Aunt Latrice promised me she'd tell Uncle Red the trouble had ended. I stood weak-kneed, almost unable to stand on my own two feet. I called Penny's beeper next and left Aunt Latrice's number, where I planned to go as soon as I could get there, hoping to spread the good news.

This was the close of a week's worth of living hell. I looked forward to a trial, to seeing Balem Moxley led about in shackles. I looked forward to going to my place in Mount Olive and starting my life anew. I wanted it all to be made right for the peace of Baxter Parish, if the parish ever had any peace. I wondered how a stroke of luck, my getting away from Moxley almost as a coward and then having him fall prey to his own shit-heap motorcycle, would change the course of my life as clear and true as what happened when my mama's body became racked with cancer. I wondered how this final good fortune might change things in Mount Olive for the better. I also wondered about how it would affect Moxley's wife and girl.

I walked out the glass doors into the radiant heat of Thomas Jefferson Avenue, looking toward the railroad tracks and the old downtown section of Pickleyville. The traffic was heavy between the buildings and I remembered seeing a black-and-white photograph from 1909 taken where I stood. The downtown still looked the same except for the hard-surface road, red lights, and cars. The horses and the buggies were gone, sucked down the hole of the past, swallowed by progress, but the old brick buildings looked exactly the same.

Parked beside my truck was a yellow wrecker, a flatbed with Moxley's Harley-Davidson tied down on the bed. I stopped and made an inspection. The hatchets were steel, regular heads like a Boy Scout would carry on a camping trip, but they had pipes for handles tack-welded to the front forks of the motorcycle, sort of like big ears poked out each side of the front end. Gray soot covered the hatchets as if they'd been affixed hours before he left out that morning. The bike was an old panhead, perhaps from the 1960s, and it was modified some, chromed over, but in bad repair. There was the little leather bicycle seat and black leather saddlebags. A long horsetail dangled from the back fender.

I stood staring at the Harley. It bothered me that I didn't understand Moxley's line on me. I couldn't tell how he could trace my comings and goings, and I never suspected I was being followed on my way to the junior college.

Then I looked at the skull and saw the green tennis ball stuck in its mouth hole. I got a chill down my back. I looked closer at the skull and saw a tooth capped in silver, then another capped tooth, and I got away from the motorbike and the voodoo skull almost in a run.

CHAPTER 22

I drove straight to Aunt Latrice and Uncle Red's house after leaving the police station. Aunt Cat was there with them. For the time being, everything made good sense and was whole, and life was what it was supposed to be, only a lot better.

"They tell you the charges?" Uncle Red asked, his fingers holding an unlit Camel. I suppose the good news overcame any questions about my staying away at night, no doubt in their minds I'd been at Penny's place.

"No. Didn't say."

"Well, it ought to be one helluva lot of bad charges against him."

"Ought to be a whole list of charges." I told them about the skull and hatchets on the motorcycle and it gave me the goose bumps just telling it.

"Where are they going to keep him?" Aunt Cat questioned me, speaking through a haze of exhaled smoke.

"I reckon at the Pickleyville jail, downtown. Right there at City Hall."

"At least that son of a bitch Haltom Roberts won't have a damn thing to do with it," Uncle Red said.

"Haltom used to be good," Aunt Latrice interrupted.

"That was twenty-five years ago, Latrice, before his pants pockets got filled with public money. A good politician is like a good aneurysm of the brain," Uncle Red said, striking a match for his Camel. "Ain't none."

*

From the conversation with the police I figured I'd see everything turn back normal, back to the way things ought to be. When you buy yourself a piece of land, a piece of property, by God, it ought to be yours without question. I guess I believed in the American dream, the U.S. Constitution, the Bill of Rights, and the flag, and all of what I said I would uphold in June of 1977 down at Jackson Barracks in New Orleans when I was sworn in for the Army.

Sitting at the kitchen table, I thought about the threats against me, about Carlin still in the hospital. I thought about that little dog butchered. I thought about the way my fate had taken an accidental good turn toward survival earlier in the day. I thought about all the suffering in the world not too far from home that needed relief. Would Moxley's actions with Carlin be made right? Maybe now that the police had him, the Pickleyville city cops not the Baxter Parish sheriff's deputies, the law might take a look into all the bullshit, see what Moxley was into, especially with the sheriff.

After eating a tuna salad sandwich and drinking a glass of sweet tea, I got back in the truck to leave for Mount Olive, to go up and check on things, to see what I might do next to make a home out of the house and land. As I was about to pull out of the yard, Uncle Red flagged me down from the carport. I killed the motor. He walked up to the cab of the truck and looked at me through the rolled-down window.

"Jesse, you be careful up yonder. One time, years ago, old man Wally Ray Kinchen killed a big old copperhead in his garden with a shovel handle. Kind of beat the snake's body in two pieces at the middle. Old snake quit moving. Then Kinchen hung up that snake on a strand of bob-wire fence to show people when they come around. About two hours later, his shepherd dog drug it off from the wire, and brung it back up to the porch. His dog was a-snapping at it, a-barking. Making lots of racket. So Wally Ray went over yonder and slapped the dog upside the long nose and told him to shut the hell up. He grabbed up that snake to carry him over to the trash barrel. You know what happened to old Wally Ray?"

"No."

"Piddling-assed snake bit the hell out of him. Like to killed him dead. Old man lost the use of his right arm the rest of his days. You know what I'm saying?"

"All right," I said.

"Snake ain't dead before the sun goes down. Way God made snakes, I guess, and Moxley ain't dead yet. You hear?"

"Yes sir." I cranked the Chevy and drove away. I watched Uncle Red out the rearview mirror till I was on the blacktop highway and gone.

When I passed the store on Highway 38 up in Mount Olive, the country store with two gas pumps out front, where the old man seemed to know plenty about Moxley, and his ways of going about things, I observed the strangest of sights.

Pedaling into the parking lot was a woman in a thin blue dress that looked as if it was cut from an old bedsheet. It looked as if she was almost floating in air, the dress draping across the three-wheeled bike she rode, a basket on the back made of wire.

It took a few seconds to realize that it was Nokomis Moxley. She was riding a big tricycle, and it appeared from her face, the sweat drenching her neck, that she was under some great stress and strain beyond the energy it took to pedal the machine, wheels moving at a snail's pace, as if she was carrying some invisible and mighty burden.

I whipped into the parking lot and beat her to the front of the store, unsure why I was stopping. I didn't know what I was going to say to this woman, her husband in jail for trying to cut me down on his motorcycle. Maybe he'd do time in prison on account of the old house and what he'd done to me. I knew I'd be close to the source of my trouble when I spoke to her.

At the end of the parking lot, over by the little cinder block storefront, near the twin gas pumps, Nokomis stopped the tricycle. She walked toward the door.

I stared at her expressionless face. She opened her mouth to say something to me then stopped. She must have recognized me and knew my role in the arrest down in Pickleyville.

I got out of the truck, my feet on hard asphalt.

"Mrs. Nokomis," I said.

She gawked at me.

"Awh, the good-looking young man what came to my aid at the house of the Lord." She smiled.

I remembered her hand on my neck. Felt it once again in my mind. "Mrs. Nokomis." I stuttered, unsure of what to say. "You know I'm your neighbor."

"You surely the sweet one what helped me at the church. I know I'd like to be a real good neighbor to you sometime, if you'd let me." She grinned again.

I wasn't after what she was after. "Yes, I'm the one that bought Pearl Moxley's house from the bank. The old Moxley place."

She slapped her mouth shut as if she was going to stop breathing. A wrinkle of skin formed around the side of her mouth. She stepped closer to the door. Her face turned dark and she spit out these words: "Have mercy, leave today. Just downright leave. You leave. They is a foul spirit amongst that place. A many a-foul spirit. Hon, you go on. Don't look back. Remember Lot's wife. Go on, hon!" She put her hand on the door handle while still speaking to me.

"Ma'am, I'm sorry about your husband being in jail and all—"

She cut me off. "Cotton ain't in no jail, hon. He's pestering with his bulldogs. His van is broke down and he won't fix it fer me. I had to ride that cycle yonder. He's over at the house sparring his bulldogs in the yard as I left. All kinds of blood on his shirt that I'll have to bleach clean."

It was like lightning had struck me. A big bolt of lightning, and I questioned if it might not be time to get the hell out of Mount Olive.

I went directly over to the pay phone and called my cousin's law office, telling him what I just heard. How Moxley was free, or at least granted some kind of release.

Ellis said he'd look into it immediately. He ordered me to go to Packwood Corners and not to return to Mount Olive, no matter what. My cousin said he was going to see Judge Marshall and attempt to show that the restraining order was clearly broken based on the police reports in Pickleyville if he could get a copy, that the judge's order had been wantonly violated, that Moxley was willfully avoiding being served. Ellis also warned me not to drive anywhere alone.

"Jesse, you need to hear something. Listen up. Sam Bullfinch was found beat unconscious inside his office last night," Ellis said.

I was stunned. "Are you meaning it was Moxley?"

"Yes. I learned this from a Ruthberry fireman. Bullfinch has his jaw wired shut and refuses to communicate with the investigators."

"Damn."

"And Jesse," he said, "the best I can do for you as a dead man is to be your pallbearer. That won't do a soul any good, you hear?"

I heard Ellis. I was listening. I went back to the truck and sat there thinking. I fished the pistol out of the glove box, rearranging a box of shells, flashlight, and my old cuffs. I made damn sure the .38 was close by for the sake of comfort. I put my hand on it.

I saw the woman exit the store with a loaf of bread hanging out from a brown paper bag, another plastic bag dangling from her hand. She put the bag in the basket and never looked up. Her head was pointed down and she picked her leg up over the low bar. I watched her begin to pedal, starting up the incline to the blacktop, and I could see clearly that both of us had one hell of a hard row to hoe every day of our lives.

CHAPTER 23

When I got to Old Sawmill Road I found Uncle Red at his hay barn, the rusted low-hung chicken house that had been dormant for a dozen years, the hens long gone. I could almost feel the clucking of the White Leggers, thousands of them, the way they used to electrify the air with a constant grate of noise. Uncle Red kept giant rolls of hay stacked in the barn for his cows, the rolls five feet high and as wide as they were tall, a thousand pounds apiece. He was cleaning out several unused rolls from last winter.

He was seated on his red and silver tractor with the three-spike hayfork stuck out the rear end, an iron spear.

I walked close to the tractor and Uncle Red caught a glimpse of me. He nodded. He was about to remove a bale of hay from the barn with the others, but he cut the engine down to an idle. I ran a finger across my throat and he shut the motor off completely.

"Yeah," he said.

"Moxley's out of jail. Just saw his old lady up in Mount Olive. Son of a bitch is let loose."

"Damn it all to hell," Uncle Red said, a wad of chewing tobacco in his jaw. He spat. "They let him out?" Uncle Red was turning the crimson hue of his tractor.

"It appears so," I said.

"I guess it's time to put those pieces of pipe to good use. Time to go see Moxley and come to an understanding," he said.

I nodded. Then I remembered something. "The son of a bitch has a wife and little girl. We got to be sure they don't get hurt."

"We'll do our best," he said.

That didn't make me feel good. I wanted to be sure they didn't get in the middle of all of this, but I followed Uncle Red anyway. We went to his shop and loaded the wooden box of pipe bombs into the truck.

"I talked to Palestine Teal this morning. Learned something from him. Folks say that old Moxley's a goddamned child molester. I learned some other things from Teal."

"What?"

"Cotton Moxley and Haltom Roberts go way back. You remember how Haltom's first wife died in a bad wreck on 55, maybe twenty years ago?"

"No."

"Well, it was back when you was just a kid. Moxley staged the accident. You remember how that old boy Reivers was left crippled, that one running for sheriff in '76, ahead of Haltom in the run-off election?"

"I do. The man fell from a scaffold when he was painting his own house. He never would talk about it."

"Moxley did it. He's done work for Governor Edwin Edwards and them crooked-assed insurance commissioners in Baton Rouge, and about every other goddamned outlaw in this state from the post office to the pew. He's worked for just about every sumbitch what wears a expensive suit."

Uncle Red was grinding his teeth, having dislodged a bite of chewing tobacco from his jaw and thrown it to the ground. He started taking the plastic off a new pack of Camels. "This is one ramshackled horseshit mess," he said.

"It is that," I answered. "No doubt about it."

"It's worse. Only one thing makes it worse. Haltom and Moxley has the same daddy. Haltom's old man used to get around, fathered a stray colt. They wasn't raised together, but they're half-brothers, Teal says. That keeps them working together. They got blood between them."

I couldn't believe it. I was almost struck dumb. "You sure about this?" I asked.

"Uh-huh. Teal says it and I believe it makes sense."

That afternoon I went to see Penny at work. She was able to take a short break in the middle of the afternoon and we went to the hospital café to get coffee. We found a corner booth in the deserted restaurant.

I caught her up about Moxley. She was upset by the business of the man's release from jail.

"So what are you going to do?" she asked.

"That's what I wanted to talk to you about. I think I'm going to go sit it out with Uncle Red up in Mount Olive. Just kind of wait on Moxley's next move."

"You mean go wait on Moxley to come over for a shootout like in *High Noon* or something?"

I hesitated. "More or less."

"And is this your Uncle Red's idea?"

"More or less."

"Jesse, you need to let Ellis take care of this. Red Tadlock is going to get you killed."

"Perhaps."

She brought the cup of black coffee to her lips but didn't drink. She put the cup down on the table. "I thought you had changed. I thought you were your own man, like the Army had changed you. I wondered if you were going to listen to Mr. Red. You listen to him and you'll live violence—right back to Percivil Herrin and Pickleyville High and Ivy Williamson, just like when you ran away to the Army. You listen to him and you're right back in 1977."

"Well."

"Are you a leader or a follower?" she asked, now standing beside the booth, glaring at me, her cup left on the table.

My temper was beginning to rise by two notches. I was holding my tongue.

"What are you?"

I didn't answer.

"When you decide whose man you are, give me a call, but I won't be waiting on you again, that's for damn sure." She turned around and walked away through the cafeteria without looking back.

I let her go. I let her go but it tore on me enough to cause nausea and hate. I questioned whether I should follow Uncle Red's lead. I debated whether it was a greater cowardice to follow him or to walk away from Moxley. I didn't know the answer.

Later in the day, Uncle Red and I loaded some ice chests in my truck, some cots and pillows, the guns, and the explosives.

"You reckon we can stand the skunk smell?" I asked.

"Maybe." Uncle Red didn't look convinced.

There was a stack of Posted signs and tools, and a big logging chain and padlocks in the bed of my truck, plus all of the hardware we bought at Kmart.

The road north to Ruthberry was like a pathway to paradise back when I went to sign up for the job at the Sherriff's Office, the day I saw the house and land in Mount Olive, but now it was a hard burden to travel, as if turning off I-12 onto I-55 headed to the north end of the parish was a thousand mile journey. The whole way it felt like a negative power. I had to fight the wheel the whole ride up there.

Uncle Red and I took sacks of clothes, clothes enough to wear for a few days. He said that we were going to wait Moxley out, to draw him to us.

The tractor was out back behind my truck on a four-wheel trailer, and there were two chainsaws and five-gallon cans of fuel.

My uncle asked me if I cared to sell some trees. I said it didn't matter.

"Then we'll eat his ass up with the trees and the chainsaw," said Uncle Red. "One tree at a time."

From what I could figure, Uncle Red was not going to depart from Mount Olive till he killed Moxley. I was less committed. I would have been happy to just get the bastard to leave me alone. Just leave me the hell alone would be plenty good enough for me. Now I was in the shits with Penny and in between a rock and a hard place all the way around.

Back in the Army, I took on the view that two opposing forces, negatives and positives, could not only coexist, but could be essential in the game of producing the right energy, whether with the charge of a battery producing light, or the Russians and Americans existing for each other's survival. Perhaps without the two forces, there could be neither life nor prosperity for either group. To will ourselves alone, naturally, would mean our own destruction, to will our own annihilation.

I came to believe that Moxley wasn't this kind of thinker. He was the kind that doesn't care about peace or life, nor about the coming judgment or even karma. Likewise, I was sure that Uncle Red wasn't the kind of person to let it all go, to let it pass, not at this point in the struggle. Hell no, he wasn't this kind of man in the least. There were times when I wished I hadn't involved Uncle Red, because the stakes were such that they couldn't be walked away from now.

When we arrived at the house, Uncle Red took a smoke from a Camel, sitting there on the porch in his overalls. He had a scowl on his face, and the .45 auto was hanging from his right overalls pocket. It was loaded just like my revolver.

The skunk scent was only in the air when you walked through the unlocked door to the house. It was almost bearable. It was a strong musk smell, not nearly as bad as when we were there before.

We unloaded the two duffle bags and the folding chairs from the truck, the ice chests, too. The house looked like an old hunting camp in the woods, very little furniture.

We ate sardines out of little tins, two cans apiece with saltine crackers. Aunt Latrice sent a jar of pickled pigs feet and we ate one foot apiece, the vinegar opening my nasal passages, making my nose run slightly. We drank the sweet tea she sent in a gallon glass jar.

Then we changed the locks on the doors again. When we were finished, we went out to the property line and nailed up fifty Posted signs, orange letters on a black background, nailed them to fenceposts and trees. I kept the M16 handy as we put up signs from one end of the property to the other.

We stretched a logging chain across the gap opening at the road, near the cattle guard, looping one end of the chain around a big hole in a creosote railroad timber post and padlocked it.

I had a strong sense of what was to come. I loved Uncle Red and knew him like no other man, but I worried about the danger he was getting us into, one step closer to destruction.

We ran a circle of wire around the house, about forty feet out, trip-wires, using the heavy monofilament fishing line. We fastened the detonators to the pipes. Near the pipe bombs, stuck in the ground almost six inches, we ran the steel wires. The bombs looked like sticks stuck out of the ground, like heads without bodies, secure in the earth. At the grassed-over gravel road, we left a gap so we could pass through to drive to the house.

I was apprehensive about the caps detonating the bombs by accident. I told Uncle Red about my concern.

"They're pull-caps. When they get pulled in any direction, 180 degrees, with twenty pounds of pressure, they go off. Not easy to do without being a booby, why they call 'em booby traps. Blow that booby-assed shitbird through the air. I figure they'll either kill the bastard or let us know where he's been, and we'll have to shoot him, run him down.

"One thing we got to do yet," he pointed to the surroundings, "cut us enough trees to piss him off. Them trees are green gold, and they'll cause him to come out the shadows," Uncle Red said. "And it'll also make you a little money until work starts."

So we did just that. We started select-cutting pines throughout the place and then stripping them of their sap-filled limbs, cutting them into sixteen-foot saw log sections, and dragging them to the front of the place at the road with the tractor. We cut down two good trees before dusk, the chainsaw winding out into the resin and thick bark, the sap nearly gumming the saw bar.

Uncle Red felled the trees and I cut the limbs, never straying far from the rifle.

I could imagine Moxley popping his head out of the woods and me aiming at his beard just like a pop-up target in basic training, dropping the man dead as a sack of potatoes.

I was getting tired, sweat seeping straight through my brown Army-issue T-shirt. We snagged the last log of the day to the road. I walked behind the tractor, the chain attached to the log by a cant hook.

"Son, how are you doing with money?"

"Not good. Down to three hundred-fifty bucks."

"I bet you got about three hundred dollars here. We'll carry it to the mill at Greensburg tomorrow."

"If there is a tomorrow," I said.

"There'll always be a tomorrow."

"I spent about all my money on the pickup and this place. You reckon the bank'll take it back with all the trees gone, assuming that's the only resolution?"

"To hell with the bank. You spending all your cash was a mistake. You ought'n done that. Should have financed it. Then the bank would have a problem, too. You could tell them you ain't paying the god-damned note. You ain't got what you paid for is why. Let the banker screw around with Moxley. Now you're on your own."

"I guess I got your help. That doesn't make me on my own."

"Well, I suppose you're right," he said.

Back at the house, in the kitchen, we baked a whole hen in barbecue sauce made mostly from brown sugar and mustard and bourbon and ketchup. Cooked it in the gas oven, letting it bake in the sauce, the hen wrapped in aluminum foil for an hour's time.

While it cooked, we went out into the perimeter near the house, and finished zigzagging the lines around the yard as close as fifty feet to the house, then connecting them to the already hot line. There were nearly two-dozen pipe bombs, so the lines were stretched a good distance between the pipes, the lines propped up with stakes made from one-by-one pinewood we'd brought. The lines were two deep, and the monofilament ran connectors between stakes and bombs. To avoid stepping on a wire might enliven a man, give him some confidence, but soon he'd trip into the other line and would be hit with shrapnel. I suppose a raccoon or a dog could even trip it. Blow the animal to pieces. Knowing the danger, my heart was in my throat the entire time while we set the bombs, breathing as hard and deliberate as a man with emphysema.

Uncle Red used aluminum clips to fasten the lines to the detonator caps, clips that fastened like hooks with snaps. The clips attached the fishing line to the stainless steel liter wires, and the liters were clipped with a ring to the pipe bombs.

The day's hard labor was wearing me down, compounded by the risk of it all; I was so tired I could hardly see straight.

After an hour of this, we went back inside and ate. The supper tasted good, and we split the meaty chicken in half and ate it with slices of white bread. We ate supper at the round cedar table we'd pulled inside the screen porch, eating the food with relish. We drank one beer apiece.

Uncle Red and I sat in front of the thirteen-inch TV Mama owned, the boob tube, one of the few things the skunks didn't ruin, or the coyote didn't break in the struggle. We watched a rerun of a movie called *Southern Comfort*, a story about a National Guard unit somewhere in the Louisiana swamps doing battle with a bunch of nutty-assed Cajuns. We watched the show seated in a couple of plastic chairs we'd brought for this very purpose. The movie kind of reminded me of us.

I sat there thinking about how Moxley hadn't shown his face all day, but I had a sense that he knew our every move. At times I reasoned that he surely knew better than to get himself blown to bits by a tripwire attached to a homemade bomb, same way he avoided getting shot between the eyeballs by the people who had plenty of reason to kill him in the past. Moxley knew all about this business as a long-time player in the game of death, and he'd obviously done well just to stay alive.

CHAPTER 24

We talked more than normal throughout the evening at the house, there in front of the TV set, Uncle Red asking me about what all I did in the Army, about Germany and Puerto Rico, Japan, about the different bases I'd been stationed at while in the United States, the people I met while gone for twelve years.

There was the steady hum of the box fan in the window, the buzz full and low, a mist in the air. I always liked the sound of a big window fan, and maybe that was the real reason I bought the place: the box fan setting dormant in one window. It's strange how something as simple as an old box fan that's no longer made can draw you to itself, bringing you into a feeling of home. The old fan was three feet wide. The blades reminded me of giant fig leaves, spinning faster than the eye could follow, the sharp wooden blades able to chop off a finger.

"Tell me about Daddy." I said. I last saw him when I was three years old, and remember almost nothing.

"Ernest was a good kid. He picked strawberries and peppers for Vincent Santangelo; he worked all the time, even when he was just a little feller, maybe ten years old. He was taller than you but not as heavy, six-three or better, hundred seventy-five pounds. Ernest rode a Appaloosa gelding all over God's creation, a horse named Bald, and he owned a Catahoula dog named Moon, and that cur was always right there at his stirrup trotting along as big as you please.

"When he met your mama, Helen, he was some in love with her.

Goodness. You'd see Ernest in his pickup with Helen sitting so close it looked like a single head in the windshield instead of two, and that was back when a boy couldn't hardly take a girl for a spin in his car alone.

"But there wasn't nothing we could do in 1962. He joined before we could stop him. With a young kid he might have avoided the draft altogether. I'd been drafted to Korea and knew what the hell it was about. That Faller boy was hard of hearing, and the Smithpeters kid with a bad leg. They didn't have to go, both 4F. Your daddy just went and joined up for the hell of it, got stuck in Uncle Sam's Army like a flea on a dog's mangy ass.

"You know, I might have drove him to Canada if he'd wanted me to. Damn, he went and joined. It wasn't right to chase the globe looking for gooks under Kennedy and later under that big-eared Johnson. Ernest was a good boy. Damn shame he never really got to know you."

I sat there thinking about the way he died. I just wasn't old enough to remember him. All I had was a picture of Daddy in my head from a photograph taken after boot camp, smiling white-faced and slim and bright-eyed. I wasn't but four when he passed on.

"I thank you for looking out for us over the years, especially after Uncle Roy died."

"That's what needed to be done and that's what we did. I just never wanted to lose another son."

I looked away from him. "Well, I thank you."

The TV played the movie but we didn't watch it anymore, not really. I guess we both stared into our own history, looking for something in memory's closet to make sense of the last thirty years.

"You reckon we'll hear from Moxley tonight?" I asked.

"Hard to say with that damn lunatic. Hard as hell to say."

We drifted off to the cots. They weren't really beds, though they were far better than Army cots. The cots were steel with wire springs and three-inch thick mattresses, and they'd roll up into two, fold in half.

The fan hummed and buzzed and I was asleep in ten minutes, a thin cotton sleeping bag pulled over me. Before I knew it, I fell away into the parting of night.

At about eleven o'clock the phone rang in the kitchen. I got up, throwing off the sleeping bag, and ran into the room, the fourth ring by the time I made it to the phone.

"Help! Somebody's outside on the carport," the voice said. It took me a second to tell who it was. "I got my gun."

"Aunt Latrice?"

"Jesse, I've called the law. Y'all come down here quick."

Uncle Red was behind me by then and he grabbed the phone out of my hand. He ordered her to shoot through the door if she needed to.

We gathered up the guns and put on our clothes and left in my truck. Luckily we'd unhitched the trailer earlier in the day. We slowed only to unlock the chain at the gap. Then it was blowing through Stop signs and two red lights in Mount Olive.

Driving ninety, I was lost in the white lines of the interstate. We were down I-55 in twenty minutes, off I-12 to Packwood Corners in five more. Uncle Red was quiet, smoking one cigarette after another.

I pulled into the drive at the house just after the blue lights turned in before us. Smiley Pearce, a neighbor who was also a deputy sheriff, walked around the house taking a look. Pearce wore a flannel shirt, it loose around his waist, and a revolver was stuck in the small of his back.

It seemed as if someone had jerked the latch off the screen door. That much was clear. Aunt Latrice was outside with her .410 break-barrel shotgun in the crook of her arm. She was untouched, fine.

I guess we were all sort of happy. Then everyone looked at Aunt Latrice. "Oh, God," she said. "What about Cat?"

CHAPTER 25

The four of us, Uncle Red, Aunt Latrice, Smiley Pearce, and I went in two different vehicles over to Aunt Cat's house on Delmar. I rode with Pearce. We drove full throttle the half mile to Aunt Cat's, tire smoke billowing out the rear end of the police cruiser. Uncle Red and my aunt were in their green Ford sedan, the closest of their automobiles to the driveway. They were following behind us.

I could see that the side door on Aunt Cat's house was open when we pulled into the drive, and her Thunderbird was parked under the carport. Right then I envisioned things I shouldn't have been able to see. A white spot crossed in front of my eyes, a yellowish light. I saw Moxley's face in the yard. It was like a ghost or a spirit, his long white beard and pointed face mocking. I swallowed the dry spit in my mouth, looking into nothing at all, realizing it was nothing, hoping that it was nothing, knowing it was nothing, but then I saw Aunt Cat's bloated head stuck on one of my fence posts up in Mount Olive, out near the main road, staring out at me when we pulled up into her drive. The woman's eyes were stuck open.

I shook all of a sudden, rubbed the sleep out of my eyes, and saw that I was in Packwood Corners, not Mount Olive. "Goddamn it," I said. I scrubbed my hands across my face as if to take away the image from my mind.

As we exited the car and went to the house, the deputy didn't say a word. Pearce stopped me at the door. "Keep them from coming in here and don't touch nothing or let them touch a thing." He entered the house with his pistol drawn, the weapon pointed in front of him.

I went back to the cars and stopped Aunt Latrice and Uncle Red at the Ford. Aunt Latrice was crying and moaning and whimpering, harsh sounds coming from inside the car.

"Cat is dead. Cat is dead. She's dead and gone," Aunt Latrice cried.

There wasn't any comfort when the deputy came out of the house, a grave contortion on his face, morose like he'd visited the same watching head I saw on the fence post in my morbid dream.

It was the insanity of violence that we bought and paid for, as if we needed it to live. To eat and drink violence and pain to know we were still alive. I couldn't comprehend it.

"Stay off the carport. This here is a crime scene," Pearce said.

Soon the night was lit up like July fireworks, blues and whites, the sirens and flashers. At the beginning, I thanked God for the troopers from the state police. Without the state boys, I worried Haltom Roberts might bury it all like he buries everything else, avoided, postponed, silenced.

"Do y'all have anybody you suspect would want to abduct Catherine Tadlock? Anybody with cause?" one trooper asked.

"Hell yeah," I said. "Cotton Moxley of Mount Olive, Louisiana."

Nothing was determined to be missing. It appeared that Aunt Cat hadn't struggled; the door was left unlocked or picked or opened without the slightest fight.

The troopers took over the scene, and said they'd pay Moxley a visit. Then it was pointed out that this was only a missing-person case, and to question Moxley at this juncture could be a violation of his civil rights.

We were getting frustrated, and Smiley Pearce even seemed pissed-off. What went on next was like sifting around poisonous snakes in a giant colander.

A young trooper named McKigney with deep black eyes told Uncle Red that it was strictly a missing-person case, and how we all ought to go on home.

Uncle Red began to tap the officer's badge with his index finger. I stood between them, hoping to prevent my uncle's arrest. The neighbor-deputy, Pearce, stopped it before it got started, taking Uncle Red for a walk, back to the cruiser.

Larry Dix, a trooper from Pickleyville I've known since high school, told McKigney to be careful. His badge would only help him after they reattach his head to his neck.

The state troopers could find no reason to think Aunt Cat had been abducted, though they did have reason to believe someone might have jerked the screen door open sometime in the recent past. At Uncle Red and Aunt Latrice's house, there was similar evidence of damage to the door. The deputies thought some of the marks on Aunt Cat's door, fresh cuts around the knob, looked a little strange, but were really inconclusive. The best guess was that no one broke into Aunt Cat's house, they said. The fact that Aunt Cat's car was in the drive, and the lights on and the TV left playing inside the living room, the door unlocked, caused only slight concern to the officers.

I listened to the debate while Uncle Red and Pearce got their bearings at the patrol car parked in the drive, the blue lights spinning. I didn't know what to think. I just didn't know. There was no resolution, and after another half hour, the troopers said we needed to wait a day before any real action could be taken in searching for her.

I pleaded with them to go see Moxley before the woman was gone for good. Then I went through the whole history of the property dispute with the troopers, the threats, and the incident at Lake Tickfaw, and the trouble at the junior college. The troopers told me to hire a good lawyer.

"Officer Dix," I said, "Clarence Darrow couldn't help a dead man out of a parking ticket, and a good lawyer can't help me."

The trooper gave me his card, slapped me on the back, got into his cruiser, and drove out to the blacktop highway.

Pearce said we needed to be patient. He offered to take me to Uncle Red's to get some clean clothes, and I agreed.

When we got to Uncle Red's, Deputy Pearce said that he would stop by at daylight to see if Aunt Cat had turned up. I knew we were right back where we'd started, without any help from the law, and I felt too scared to hunt Moxley down and kill him like a dog. But I also knew we needed to do something.

Uncle Red and Aunt Latrice rode alone, and he later told me out in the yard that she cried all the way home, and the emotion of it made me wipe my own eyes, looking out into the darkness at his house.

It took a few minutes at Uncle Red's to check the guns for bullets, to put on some fresh clothes, to brew coffee, and then to get ourselves back into the pickups.

Though I didn't know what Penny might say to me now after our meeting at the hospital, I called her while still at Uncle Red's. It was midnight and the phone was busy. Right away I wondered if she'd found herself in the company of another man. The sorrow I felt was severe, and I was overcome with regret.

We convoyed in both our trucks to a cousin's house, Wilton Carter, a nephew over by the brickyard pond. I never got out of my truck while Uncle Red took Aunt Latrice to the raised porch of the double-wide trailer. Uncle Red met me at my Chevy where I was sipping some coffee.

"Son, let's go to Moxley's place first. See if we can get a hold of him.

Challenge him to come outside and fight. If need be, I'll say he pulled a gun on you, that I went to the truck, got my pistol and had to shoot him, assuming he doesn't tell us what we want to hear. Once they find Cat—alive or dead—they won't waste time fretting over the body of a no-good bastard."

I knew Penny had made her point and that Uncle Red was acting nuts. Even I could see this. I thought of the pipe bombs set in Mount Olive. I was already in too deep. "Why don't we go back to my house first? See if he might have come calling."

"No, we need to let him know we ain't scared, then maybe go back to your house."

"OK," I said.

As we headed out, I worked on the coffee, drank sips while driving along I-55. I ran through all of the options in my head, and none seemed real good.

CHAPTER 26

We left from the house trailer like time finally caught up to us, in a hurry to drive north. It was a kind of deserted dead-end road to nowhere, this place we were headed. In the two pickup trucks, my lead this time, I saw no ability, no way to know what to do or where to go or when this way of living would come to a close.

I felt a wild adrenaline rush earlier, heartbeat high and constant, but then it slowed despite the coffee I sipped. As I shifted gears, flying onto Highway 190, I felt sorry over how I dragged others into all of this trouble. We were in it earnest now, headed to Mount Olive like a hundred fighting monkeys in a barrel of darkness, the lid tight as a drum, plenty of arms and elbows, utter chaos. Penny's words were ringing in my ears.

I turned on the radio. A screaming preacher broadcast on the AM station up in Ruthberry, a man who hacked and sucked air each time he delivered a line. He preached as if each syllable might be his last word at the great throne of judgment. "Every road, ah-hah, must end, ah-hah, every concrete road, ah-hah, every spiritual road, ah-hah, will end, ah-hah, and the road you're on, ah-hah, is the wrong road. The Lord God Almighty, ah-hah, ain't no blind man, ah-hah. He can see real good, ah-hah. He's got, ah-hah, 20-20, ah-hah, eyes, ah-hah, day and night. He knows you, ah-hah. He knows all y'all slipping away, ah-hah, like a boat, ah-hah, in a hurricane."

I listened to the preacher for about a minute and turned off the self-confident baritone, the voice of a fire insurance salesman trying to offer a way out of hell. I drove into the lights of oncoming cars, the few that were on the highway at this time in the morning.

At seventy-five miles an hour, I was ten above the speed limit on the interstate. The M16 was beside me, the .38 loaded and resting on the seat. The .22 magnum with the scope was behind the seat. My house in Mount Olive was encircled with wires of death like a pit of cobras.

I owed Aunt Cat. She'd fed us when we had no money to buy groceries. She and Uncle Roy took us in when we were kicked out of houses a time or two for falling behind on monthly rent. She propped us up till Uncle Red and Aunt Latrice's house came available, when a great-aunt died back a couple years before I graduated from high school.

All of what I knew of safety and salvation came from the hands of these people, my aunts and uncles in Packwood Corners. Aunt Cat was gone, gone into the hands of a madman named Moxley. All over a piece of land less than two football fields wide and four football fields long, an old house in poor repair, a house battered by a hundred years of wind and rain. I asked why I would risk them all for it. I asked right then if I was apeshit crazy as Moxley, if it wasn't a fool's errand to start with? I couldn't tell, but Penny had warned me about this.

Somewhere about Ruthberry I started to nod off and could hardly stay awake, but by the time I exited 55 onto Highway 38 at Mount Olive, I was awakened again when I saw an image of death in the truck, a dark shadowy image that took over the cab for a few seconds, just unquestioned fear. It awoke me like fire. Not that I was in dread or in awe of dying, though I didn't know at that moment how God would take to my life as it was, as little and as pointless as it was. There was a terror over what might be, the state of Aunt Cat in the no-man's land of Mount Olive. It got to me, unsettled me even more.

Uncle Red flagged me down, flashing his high beams when we turned down Spears Road. I slowed, watching his lights flashing from high to low. He pulled up close behind me, his chrome bumper touching my rear bumper.

He hurried to my truck. "Have we got cause to think going in there on Moxley will hurt Cat more'n she's got to be hurt already?" he asked from my window.

"Not as I can tell," I said. That's not what I should have told him. I gripped the pistol with my right palm on the seat, sort of a constant squeeze.

"All right. You keep straight down the road ahead of me, and I'll hang close behind you. Don't take your lights off of high beam. Go on to Moxley's place. If he comes out with a gun, I'll shoot him. Don't let the bastard get out of his yard without firing. If he runs and I can't hit him, you shoot him. Just aim at a leg. Maybe you can wing him."

"I got an M16. I might kill him," I said.

"Well, 'fore he dies at least we might get him to tell us where she's at."

"There's a woman and a kid in the house. I ain't got no cause to harm them. I don't want to see them hurt is what I'm saying."

"Then hit him square in the chest and they won't be no stray bullets flying around. The bullet'll stop where it needs to stop."

For longer than was comfortable, I stared at Uncle Red. The worry lines were deep across his forehead. The years of living a few steps behind progress, the ways of fighting the whole world, had caught up to him, in that very second, I believe.

"Sure," I said.

"Be careful."

"I will."

*

Rut holes covered the gravel lane off Spears Road, holes deep enough to bend an axle on a car. In spite of this, I drove as fast as I could, knowing that the longer I drove, the more chance Moxley would hear of our arrival, the more time he'd have to prepare. The beat-up gravel road ran a half mile or more, snaking way behind my place, and it looped itself around to the logging road where Nokomis and the girl made me bring them one Sunday after church.

Trees were all the way up to the road, wedging in the logging road to the house. Uncle Red's truck followed close behind from the sound of it as I banged in and out of the ruts. His lights jumped and flashed into my rearview mirror, the truck so close behind was Uncle Red's way of saying, "Be careful." Or maybe it was his way of saying, "We're in this together." An occasional limb would slap the windshield of my pickup and scrape all the way down the bed making a screeching noise.

When I pulled into the little clearing, I could hear the dogs tune up and the chickens crow. The noise was loud in the cab above the mufflers and the tires banging in and out of the ruts. No telling what all lurked in the shadows.

I stopped the truck. I opened the door, reaching for the M16. I was half in the truck, half out, the door open in front of me like a shield. I shifted the rifle into my left hand and pressed down on the truck horn till it was beeping, taking its place amidst the sounds of dozens of dogs and cocks making a racket. All of this commotion would have caused anyone inside the house to think of Gabriel's horn at the Last Judgment.

Kill. Kill. Kill the son of a bitch that's killed your kin. Kill the no-good bastard. My mind spoke to me like the words of God himself. My right hand took the M16 and I sensed the hair rise on my neck. The horn blasted. Uncle Red's lights blazed behind me and I could barely hear both our truck motors amid the animal chaos.

Whether it was two or three minutes, I do not know, but the house was silent and dark, not even as much as a porch light turned on, just the pickup's high beams spraying the place with a silver glow.

Finally a light came on inside the house and I drew the weapon to my shoulder and pointed it down at the bottom of the porch, ready. The door opened. It was the woman, Nokomis, standing there in the door among the gloom of the ragged porch; she wore a nightdress that left a crease between her breasts clear and inviting.

"Awh, can I help you?"

"Where's your old man?" I shouted above the barking and crowing sounds.

The woman pulled her hand up to her eyes. She rubbed her brow. "He's gone. Been gone since last night. Probably fighting one or another of his bulldogs, or visiting one or another of his dry cows."

I could hear the tone of her voice, and I favored her words in an instant. I felt the metal of the gun, and realized I was massaging the trigger a half-ounce too hard.

"Where the hell is he?" I heard Uncle Red scream, saw his shadow come up beside me, his rifle like a limb in the truck light.

Nokomis cupped her hand over her eyes to fight the glare. "Cotton said he was going to South Carolina to fight his dogs. Don't know more'n that. Who's out there?"

I believed she was telling the truth as she knew it, but I also knew that Moxley hadn't gone too far.

"Woman, don't lie to me," I heard Uncle Red holler out.

"I ain't got no idea where he's off to. I'm his old lady, not his keeper."

"She's telling the truth," I said.

"You reckon she is?"

"Hell yeah. She's saying what she knows. But I bet the bastard's around close by."

"Then let's go find his crazy ass."

I got back into the truck and the woman went inside the house, the front door shutting behind her. I managed to turn around in the junky yard without hitting anything, killing an animal, as did Uncle Red. I followed him back down the logging road, back into the places of the unknown.

The moon was hidden behind a roof of clouds, leaving the pitch-dark night. Night has never seemed as black in my life. The humidity crept into my bones and made sweat bead above my cheeks and drain down the corners of my eyes.

There was a great letdown after Nokomis came out and said her husband was gone. The frankness of her voice, the way she said her words in a manner without need to convince. Just to tell it, that nothing could be sillier than to doubt what she said.

While I was driving, fighting the ruts, I questioned for the first time whether Aunt Cat was really snatched away. It all made very little sense, no sense to my thinking. Moxley was gone, maybe long gone. Impossible that he'd risk heading to south Baxter Parish to do his mixing of trouble with good air, but I didn't know what to think. Uncle Red was ready to kill a man, and if a man needed killing. Moxley needed taking down.

Within Moxley's nature was a heart set on my destruction, an allegiance within himself to cause me harm. Just the love of death at its core, I believe, was what he was after.

"That would do it," I said to myself. "Killing the son of a bitch would do it."

I crossed my cattle gap and heard the thud-thud-thud sound beneath the truck tires, front and back. My headlights shined a cottontail rabbit at the edge of the grassy road.

The house was dark, and I noticed the front light on the porch must have blown. The light was on four hours earlier, before we fled the place in a fever to see about Aunt Latrice. I distinctly remembered leaving the light on, and seeing it in the rearview mirror as we left the house heading to Packwood Corners.

I crossed the opening of the trip wire perimeter, wishing for nothing but a little peace, maybe some word my aunt was OK. I inched up near the side of the house at the carport, killing the headlamps, rolling up the window. I figured it would be easier to turn on the lights at the screen porch than to go inside, but the porch had a latch on the inside. Then I realized that maybe a breaker tripped or blew because the screen porch light wasn't on either.

Uncle Red pulled in behind me, and I could see the orange glow of his cigarette in the darkened cab. I was making a trip to the front porch with guns and some bags. The key was in my hand. When I was almost back to the truck I thought I saw a pair of steely eyes inside the screen porch door. I jerked the pistol out of my belt, and cocked the hammer back, the hard click stinging the night sounds.

As I looked more closely, the eyes were not inside the door. Fatigue was getting to me. There were no eyes at all as I took a step, or two steps away from the door, backing away like a crawfish moving into a corner.

Uncle Red drew his pistol and was up beside me pointing it.

"I just thought I saw something," I said. A sense of unease overcame me about this, something totally wrong, the way it must have felt to step on a claymore mine like my daddy did, knowing that any movement down or up would be the end. Hairs were rising and falling on my forearms as if I'd slipped unwillingly into a field of energy.

"Good God," Uncle Red said, his breath near my neck.

I still pointed the revolver at the door, leveled it at the screen porch. My finger longed to pull the metal trigger. The pistol bounced with each heartbeat as I stared down its steel sight. I lowered it to the ground.

Uncle Red shone his flashlight. I knew I was seeing things.

"Nobody's in there," I said.

The tension crowded me with all that had happened for a week, all the harassment, the attempt of murder with the motorcycle, and my Aunt Cat's disappearance. I didn't think clearly. I reacted. I looked hard to see something, someone I wanted to face down.

But my ears were not ringing. The gun did not buck. I uncocked it and slipped it into my belt.

The truck headlights were still left on, so we could see to get inside the house. "Jesse, what you reckon's wrong with the lights?" Uncle Red asked.

"Breaker's blowed, probably."

"Where's the box at?"

"Over on the wall, right up by the door on the screen porch," I said. We were standing under the carport. I turned around to get something from the truck and Uncle Red went toward the screen porch. It didn't occur to me to stop him, to tell him that the door was latched from the inside.

Uncle Red walked up the steps, pistol in his belt and flashlight in his left hand. "Let's shed some light on the subject." He opened the door.

At that moment, I wondered how I could avoid killing the son of a bitch Moxley. My head was pounding and I heard Penny's pleas in my ears. I wasn't thinking straight.

I wanted to know what happened to Aunt Cat even if it was too late to help her. I wanted a little justice. Just a little justice. No matter,

I wanted peace too. The clamor of voices in my head didn't want either.

Then I heard a breaker flip, the crack of the breaker and a shriek, an awful blood-filled scream from the porch, a goddamned buzzing scream. Screaming like nothing I'd ever heard before.

"Gawwhh—gawwh—gawwhh," sounds came from the porch. Sounds and sparks and fire shooting from the wall near the screen, light falling in arcs of silver behind the wire mesh.

I jumped up the concrete steps to the door and I could see Uncle Red on fire, his hand gripping the board at the wall as if he were holding a handle, blue flame shooting from the wall toward him. I froze.

This man was burning alive, burning to his death. Uncle Red's left hand held the flashlight about shoulder high as if conducting music, and his other hand was stuck out in front at the breaker box. He rode the stream of spitting current as I saw him dance. My mouth opened wide as Uncle Red jumped to the jolts of electricity at the box.

"Grahh-grahhh-guarr," my uncle wailed.

I forgot about Aunt Cat or any fear of dying. I slammed through the screen door. I bent down low at the waist and hit Uncle Red square after two leaping strides, damn near flying from the wood floor, sinking my shoulder into his flesh. I was trying to take him off the electric current in one blow, like tackling a runner to the ground near the line of scrimmage. The landing stung, bone-jarring hard on the pine floor. I smelled the charred flesh and burned hair for the first time. I realized I was atop a pile of human limbs, limp body parts, burning meat underneath me. The box kept sparking, shooting flame over us. I looked down and saw a hole in Uncle Red's side and another in his temple, and I felt a fissure form in the palm of his hand. I did not know if he had any life left in him.

I grabbed Uncle Red's feet, his boots, and pulled him, dragging him through the door and down the steps as fast as I could, nervous that the turpentine-rich pine wall might catch fire. I dragged him to the front bumper of my truck. There weren't any noises save the sparks and flames at the breaker box, and the sound of Uncle Red's skull banging the steps as we went down them together. It was as if the house would erupt with fire in seconds.

I reached and felt Uncle Red's neck for a pulse, massaging it as best I could, hoping upon hope. I could feel little if anything but his wet skin. No pulse.

No goddamned pulse. I felt Uncle Red's neck again and panic set in. I went to the truck and cranked it, thinking I could take him somewhere, God knows where. Maybe McComb and the hospital, maybe Pickleyville. I couldn't think. At the same time I realized, the man is dead.

I came back to him, remembering I'd been trained in C.P.R., the thought arising from nowhere. I bent over Uncle Red and squeezed his nose, blew into his mouth and lungs with my warm air, and then began pressing his chest like I was taught and counting. Then blow. Then press. I tasted the sweat in his mouth, the blood. It tasted of burned meat. I was screaming for help there in the woods. I was screaming for God to make an exception and do something. Press. Blow. After a minute Uncle Red coughed, the first indication that he was still alive, a nasty choking cough, but a sound made by a man alive, at least barely alive. He gasped and I loaded him into the truck cab hoisting him by his shirt and shoulders, his legs stiff.

If things couldn't be worse, out of the corner of my eye I saw something move and a slam as hard as a baseball bat hit my side at the ribs, throwing me to the ground away from the idling truck.

Fangs were in my leg, stuck in my blue jeans. My left ear heard a guttural growling as a beast chewed on my leg, its teeth keeping me down. I felt heat and water and hair and ivory. I felt the animal's legs and shoulders as it bit the back and side of my leg. The growling and chewing. The long tongue of pain. Suffocating pain and blood. I clawed. It was a dog or wolf, or a bear or a panther. I did not know. I couldn't see in the dark.

A goddamned bulldog, I realized. I had clarity to know this, what was happening to me.

I swear I heard from behind. "Roscoe, get him, boy. Kill him. Get ye some. Get him, Roscoe. Get him, boy," and laughing. Laughter and hooting and hollering, a squalling of laughter from a man, on his knees laughing like wild.

Grabbing, struggling, I found the razor-edge Buck knife on my belt. I ripped it into the dog's face, carving it as blood and water splattered from its eyes and ears. Then I started jamming it into his chest, poking it into the dog's lungs. I didn't stop till I felt the dog release.

I heard cackling around me till the bulldog fell away; the laughter stopped. I was mostly OK after the attack except the dog had ripped my pants leg off to the knee with a great slash, more pants than flesh, the worst pain coming at impact.

Then I did my best to get Uncle Red completely into the cab of the truck. As I backed away, I saw the lump of a brown dog lying in the drive.

CHAPTER 27

Most of the way to Ninth Ward Hospital I didn't know if Uncle Red was breathing or not, his breathing sometimes inaudible. I just drove as fast as I could, my eyes peeled open, my prayers questioning and pleading, begging for him to stay with me.

Uncle Red looked like the empty hull of a man, and I noticed blood draining on my seat from the holes in his wrists and side. The electric smell was awful as we flew to Pickleyville.

I had time to think. It was amazing how clear my thoughts came during the ride. I could see how I'd been sucked into this whole thing because of my longing for home and the odd-crazy way Uncle Red desired justice and vengeance with equal fervor. It all pulled me, drew me into the darkness the minute I returned to Baxter Parish. Once in, I wasn't wise enough to get out, and here was a dead man or a nearly dead man in the cab of my truck as a testament to my foolish lack of judgment.

The hospital was about a mile off of I-12 and I floored the pedal getting there. I questioned if my house was burning in Mount Olive, the end of the struggle. I didn't dare turn the electricity off, didn't dare touch the box. Maybe Moxley would be happy with a dead man and a torched house. Maybe this ended my quest for a house and land, too.

I doubted Aunt Cat's survival as I turned into the hospital drive. What happened to the woman? Where was she? Was Moxley involved?

Moxley rigged my breaker box. He was an electrician, but there was just too much happening in a single night for one bad-ass to be behind it all.

Uncle Red didn't move. I spoke to him again. I hadn't heard a gasp in a while, since about Liberty City on I-55. I looked over at him in the lights at the hospital. His lips were blue.

I pulled under the ER overhang. I thought about Penny and I wished she were there with me. It was dark outside and no one was stirring, just a handful of cars in the lot. It was five a.m.

The truck motor still running, my uncle in the cab, I ran through the glass doors and hollered at an attendant seated at a big desk. I hollered for help, saying I had a dying man in the truck outside. A moment later, Penny met me at the truck, thank God.

"Uncle Red's been electrocuted," I said.

Then came this swarm of people, doctors and nurses and orderlies. Uncle Red was on a gurney and passed the double doors in a flash. He was gone from sight, gone from my eyes, into the arms of Penny Nesom and the rest of the people paid to do something to help.

I went over to the phone and called Wilton, let him know what happened and where we were. He was still mostly asleep but said they'd be at the hospital in a few minutes. The hard waiting started the minute the call was done.

When I put down the phone, I looked at my leg and saw a ripped bloody gash. It wasn't real bad. I never felt it during the ride. I asked an orderly passing by to take a look at it, and he sent a nurse out to check on me. Later they made me fill out some papers on myself and Uncle Red.

Penny saw me out after ten minutes and told me Uncle Red was alive and that's about all. She said to phone the Sheriff's Office, which I did, reporting a possible murder attempt, a waste of breath. Penny cleaned the fresh wound on my leg with iodine. There wasn't much to the bite, the dog getting more pants leg than skin for sure.

I was still on the phone when Wilton and Aunt Latrice arrived. Initially, my aunt acted more angry than sorrowful. She was cursing her husband's foolish ways. I hugged her and she kept right on cursing him. She glared at people, as if to beg someone to offer the slightest challenge. "Y'all hid things from me," she said. "Now, by God, I want to know what happened."

Right off I told her about the night. A deputy sheriff, a Barlow from Watermelon, distant kin, stood beside me. He was there working a security detail. I made no mention of guns or pipe bombs. Thank goodness Penny came back out and saved me.

"I want to see him. How is he?" Aunt Latrice asked, not one tear in her eye.

"I'm not supposed to say, Mrs. Latrice. But it doesn't look good."

Within thirty minutes a helicopter transported Uncle Red to the Catholic hospital in Baton Rouge, and Wilton was driving Aunt Latrice there in hopes that she'd see Uncle Red again. Her only glimpse of him was when they wheeled him out to the medi-vac, his face covered in a tangle of tubes and hoses.

I settled into my story for the deputy. He listened closely to my tale—of this night and the days before. I spent some time outlining the previous weeks and the lost job and the threats and the alliance between Moxley and Roberts.

"So, what evidence do you have that Cotton was involved with this?" the deputy asked.

"It's obvious. It's more than obvious."

"Did you see anything out of the ordinary at the house when you arrived?"

I thought a second or two. Then it dawned on me. "The screen door was unlatched. It was clearly latched when we left. We left through the front door. Uncle Red just opened the side door, the screen door, and it would have been hooked from the inside when we left, no question. I should have stopped him. He went for the door not knowing it was latched or unlatched. But the thing wasn't secure any-more."

The deputy weighed matters, turned thoughtful for a moment. "Jesse, I'll go arrest Balem for trespassing if I can find him, one way or the other, and I'll see if I can get some fingerprints out at the place. Sometimes you have to bring a feller in to make things come to a head. I've been eligible to retire for six months, and I ain't worried about the trouble it might cause, bad as I hate Haltom's lies, but goddamn, you better not be shitting me about this."

"I'm not shitting anybody."

If things weren't already unreal, it got totally weird five minutes later, just as I was about to leave for Baton Rouge. Aunt Cat strolled into the ER lobby, an unlit cigarette and Zippo lighter in her right hand, her purse on her shoulder.

"What are you doing here?" I asked. Then I saw Nan walk up, Carlin's wife, and a sinking dread overtook me.

"I'm here with Nan. Carlin had a bad night and she picked me up to ride with her over here in a hurry a few hours ago."

"You didn't let anyone know."

"I said it was a hurry."

I filled her in about Uncle Red and her disappearance. From the look on her face, she couldn't believe her ears.

As I drove Aunt Cat to Baton Rouge in my pickup, she said I

should take a few things to heart.

"I know you carried a burden," she said. "You've had to carry too many burdens without a daddy and with your mama dying while you were away." She was poking at something. I knew that much. I just didn't know where she was headed.

"I ought to have done better," I said.

"How in the world, son? They said she was eaten alive with lung cancer from the start. Nothing could have stopped it."

"Maybe."

"No, you got to leave some things behind. That's something Red could never do, and I reckon you got it in your genes. You and Red's a lot alike, but you got to leave some things alone. You have to leave Mount Olive alone and let Ellis take care of it. If that don't work," she said, "leave it to the Lord."

I listened, but I didn't respond.

"And let me tell you another thing, if you don't leave it all alone, you're going to lose everything and everybody you love, more than just that place. It might be too late already. Are you hearing me yet, Jesse? You've got to leave it alone."

I drove thinking, knowing how I needed to let this one go, how I ought to let it be, but it had me like an iron trap.

CHAPTER 28

Over the next several days Uncle Red was touch and go with the burns. I spent much of my time in Baton Rouge. Penny rode over with me twice and relieved Aunt Latrice who was there day and night at Our Lady of Gethsemane Hospital. We were looking out after Uncle Red. During those trips we came to terms with each other, I suppose, kind of made up.

Deputy Barlow believed that the box was rewired, rigged, a booby trap set off when Uncle Red flipped the breaker switch. The natural effect was to ground the moment Uncle Red grabbed the breaker. He was the ground, feeling the jolt of 220 volts. The officer thought that whoever set up the box was guilty of attempted murder. He was soon told point-blank by Haltom Roberts to leave Moxley the hell alone. Barlow signed an affidavit over at Ellis's law office stating his claims.

Furthermore, Moxley was missing and could not be found for questioning about the incident, nor could he be found for possible violations of a restraining order, not that the sheriff cared about enforcing the law.

I called Ellis about the bomb perimeter. It was the morning of the electrocution and he said he would take care of it. He went up there himself and stood on the porch with a fishing rod and reel, casting a hook toward the line making all twenty-two pipe bombs explode, just casting a treble hook with a lead sinker and reeling it in, tripping the wires and picking up the scrap, the yard pitted with holes that looked like tree stumps removed with a backhoe.

After three days in the hospital, Uncle Red was finally able to talk a little, breathing on his own with the help of an oxygen mask. However, the prognosis was mixed. They said he would live only if the infections were kept under control. Pneumonia set in, and they worried about his body going septic, and he couldn't move his legs. At least he could talk at times.

I was in I.C.U. alone with him. Uncle Red pulled at his mask, his hands bandaged because of the wounds. He pushed the translucent mask to the side of his face. "Son, what are they gonna do about this?"

I told him what Barlow had said, and about the affidavit.

He looked at the ceiling, then back at me. It was as if he was cooking up a plan. It made me nervous. Heat glowed on his face in the room's light.

"That's Carlin and that's me and almost you. I'm crippled now. I'm hurt on the inside." He choked his words, and pulled the mask back over his mouth in a search for air.

"You're going to be all right." I tried to sound reassuring, positive.

"No, it ain't here no more. It's gone and I won't be getting it back."

"What are you talking about?"

"My nature, my life. I won't be worth a shit if they ever let me out of this place."

"Awh, don't talk like that."

"How else to talk?"

"Come on now."

"I just want one thing."

"Name it."

"Kill the son of a bitch Moxley. Don't do it for me, do it for the Tadlock name. We owe the no-good bastard a good killing."

I looked at him and he simply put his oxygen mask back on his face. He took several breaths, then moved it to the side of his jaw.

"You look scared?" he said.

"I can't fix anything by killing the man."

"You'll save what's left of us. You'll save us from what he done. You'll end it and pay back a bill of debt. No damned way is he done till we're all dead. I can't kill him myself. Give me your word on it," he said.

I got up from the chair and walked out of the room feeling flushed. His voice was weak in the background, and he was cursing, begging me to redeem him. I kept walking out of the I.C.U., back to my truck and on to Packwood Corners.

CHAPTER 29

I went to Aunt Latrice's house alone that night, to Murphy Jr.'s bedroom, and I felt ashamed over not being able to even the score for Uncle Red. I paced the floors and couldn't rest. I called Penny's beeper and left the number.

Penny called me shortly and I said I'd like to come by the hospital to see her.

Driving into the ER parking lot, I saw Nokomis Moxley and her little girl enter the glass doors, the woman kind of leading the waif of a child by the shoulder. The girl was beet red, almost shining.

I lagged behind, trying to avoid them if possible. I stayed in the truck and drove to another parking lot, and entered the building on the east side and went up to Carlin's room to kill some time. I did want to know what happened, the reason for them to be at the hospital, though. After visiting with Carlin, now in a double-occupancy room, his last night at Ninth Ward, I waited around for Penny at the ER. There was no sign of Nokomis and the girl, and I tried to keep a low profile.

"Hey, hon," Penny said when she saw me. I kissed her. We went out to her car.

"What's with the Moxley girl?"

"I'm not supposed to talk about it, Jesse."

"What if you just spoke to the car here and I happen to listen in on the conversation between you and the Toyota."

"Still."

"What happened?"

She leaned against her car hood. She lit a cigarette. "This is when I hate my job. The kids. People who don't live like humans."

"Come on," I said.

"Her daddy raped her. Not the first time by any means, but her mama had enough of it, and came in. The girl is ten years old and doesn't even have pubic hair yet and that asshole raped her. We did a rape kit and called the welfare department.

"The girl and her mother hitchhiked all the way to Pickleyville while Moxley was gone fighting his chickens in Hardin. She sneaked down here and now she can't go home until they arrest him; the woman is talking plenty."

I was speechless for a minute. Penny finished off the cigarette while we stood in an awkward silence.

"That's damned unbelievable." Then I remembered the rumors of Moxley being a child molester.

"You didn't hear it from me, Jesse. I could lose my job."

"Right. I didn't hear it at all."

"Why don't you get a pizza and let's watch a movie at my place. Bring some clothes. I've had enough reality for one day."

"OK. What time do you get off?"

"Six."

"I'll come by." I kissed her and held her while she leaned against the car, and I knew we both wished the world was a different sort of place.

CHAPTER 30

It was four o'clock and I drove to Aunt Latrice's, cleaned myself up and packed some clothes, and I went to town to buy a pizza. But all the while I couldn't remove my mind off Nokomis and the girl.

At Tommy's Little Sicilian Restaurant I ordered a large Greek; the aroma was of baked bread and garlic. I bought a bottle of wine on the way over to Penny's at Tidwell's Grocery, picked up a movie at the Show-to-Rent on 51. I sat on her shotgun house porch with the pizza and waited, rocking in the swing till after seven. The pizza was cold, the wine sealed. It was getting dusk dark and she should have been home an hour earlier. Uncle Red's words kept ringing in my ears: "Kill the son of a bitch Moxley. Don't do it for me, do it for the Tadlock name." The cowardice scared me, but worse, what if Moxley didn't stop till we were all dead?

At dark I became concerned and went over to my truck, got my notebook and wrote Penny a message, which I stuck in the doorjamb. I left the pizza and wine and VCR tape on the cypress swing. I drove around the corner to a gym, a health club on Old Sawmill Road that was open. I went inside and used the telephone. A man tried to sell me a membership, but I hushed him up. I beeped Penny with the gym number. I waited a few minutes and called the ER.

The guy named Terry said he'd seen her leave at six-fifteen. I panicked. I went to the truck and drove what I figured would be her path from the hospital, down Old Sawmill to 51, then up to Club Premier Road. Halfway down Club Premier I saw lights, blues and reds. Terror took over my breathing and my eyes and I watched the lights get bigger and the sirens begin to invade the Chevy cab. When I slowed the truck, I saw a blue Toyota in the ditch against a tree, and the front end was shaped like a U around the oak.

They had her on a backboard and she was bleeding from her lips. Her head must have hit the windshield. A deputy tried to stop me, the one flagging cars around the wreck, around the ambulance, but I blew by him.

"Penny," I screamed. "Penny, are you all right?"

I was at the back of the ambulance.

"I'll be OK. I'm just banged up." Her gaze was fixed on my eyes. She wore a gray neck brace.

Before I could ask what happened, she startled me with something I didn't want to hear.

"I was run off the road by a black van. I saw him, Jesse. I believe it was Moxley. He was a big man with a beard." Then she broke down and started crying, the tears running down her temples into her hair.

"Jesse."

"Yes."

"I need to tell you something right now."

I rubbed her arm. "What is it?"

"Your Uncle Red died at the hospital in Baton Rouge. Mrs. Cat called the ER before I left. I'm so sorry."

They loaded her. The sheriff's deputy told me to quit blocking the road, that I could meet them at the hospital if I wanted. When the doors slammed on the Big Cajun Ambulance, I turned around and got back into the truck like a zombie. I drove up the road a quarter of a mile and turned around, heading the opposite way from the hospital.

I felt nothing and saw nothing, as if some great wheel came out of the heavens and killed time itself. The only thing left was pain and hate circling within my soul.

CHAPTER 31

When I passed the Ruthberry exit on I-55, I knew there was no turning back. I reached over and took the handcuffs from the glove box along with my flashlight and Buck knife. "It's either me or him," I said into the air, as if perhaps God might hear it and get in the way for once, to intervene in my own death.

It was decided as simple as seeing Penny's body bruised and battered from the windshield. As simple as hearing about Uncle Red. No matter the consequence, that no-good son of a bitch would meet justice. I looked at the .38 on the seat beside me and removed Uncle Red's own Colt .45 from a cotton sack on the floorboard. Two pistols if necessary.

As I drove, I checked both of them. One was chambered and had a clip tight with steel-jackets; the other held six hollow points in the cylinder. I wasn't sick with adrenaline, wasn't worn with dread anymore. I knew it was the end and I accepted it like a man. No one would do anything about Moxley but me, no law, because he was as much a part of the law in Baxter Parish as Haltom Roberts. One way or the other, I was making a citizen's arrest or a good killing for all the torment he put people through, including Penny and the little girl.

It was dark outside on I-55 as I passed the Tangilena exit, then on past Kemp Station, on to Mount Olive, the final exit before I-55 traced its way through the state of Mississippi heading to Memphis. There wasn't even a moon in the dark sky, as clouds shrouded the night.

I parked the truck off Spears Road, about a half-mile from Moxley's place. I got out of the truck with the revolver in the front of my waist-band and the .45 in my back and the Buck knife on my belt, the cuffs looped around the knife handle, and the steel flashlight in my hand. I walked stiff and deliberate, my head set on the task. I knew the girl and her mama were down in Pickleyville, the two of them far enough from Mount Olive to avoid getting mixed up in the night's work. Then I started running down the logging road, jogging in my tennis shoes, occasionally splattering water when I hit a hole, jarring my knees but staying afoot. I remembered Uncle Red's words to avenge my kin and I ran even faster.

I ran till I left the logging road, till I slipped into the pine forests not far from Moxley's house, maybe a quarter of a mile away. My plan was to try to flank his house and come in from the side. I walked through the woods with the flashlight turned off. From time to time a dog would howl in the night, then burst into barking, and my nerves would rise into my neck. The woods were clear of brush, and I figured it was burned off recently.

Moxley's porch light shone in the distance. As I came down off a hill toward the bottom where the house was located, I could see I'd judged the distance right. I was coming from the back side of the house where the woods edged up to it. I was thankful that the dogs were kept on chains to prevent them from killing one another or killing me. For a minute or two I stood still, fifty yards from the house. I squatted and watched and listened.

A van was parked in Moxley's yard. The front glass reflected the porch light. I made out the motorcycle, chrome forks sparkling like stars at ground level.

The handcuffs were cool to the touch when I unwrapped them from around the knife handle. I opened up each cuff with the key. Then I put one cuff around my left wrist, hearing it click-click-click, setting it with the tiny key. I placed the keys in my front pocket.

Why I did this, I do not exactly know. Other than to say it was me or him, and I planned not to walk away from this, to forge justice even at the cost of my own death.

I dropped the flashlight on the ground and began rushing, twelve years of running away crowding my soul. I sprinted all the way to the porch as fast as I could, running a beeline to the front porch, running over brambles, fighting like hell to get there, always on my feet though nearly falling twice. I could hear the TV when I got to the corner of the house, and I took a long bounding jump up the side of the porch, past an old couch in the white light beside the door.

Dogs and chickens started to sound off by the time I reached the doorknob. I flung it open. It wasn't locked and I saw face-to-face how big the man Moxley was, him standing there with a beer in his hand, the tendons in his neck as big around as cigars. He was at least eighty pounds heavier than me. I hit him with an elbow and we tumbled into a chair and I grabbed one of his arms in both of my hands, clipping the cuff on his wrist, shutting it down to a sound of metal clicking. My left wrist was attached to his right wrist. All I could do was focus on this one thing as he pounded the back of my head with his fist, and I swear, it felt like a brick was in his hand, though it was as bare as a dog's paw.

He jerked me to him cursing and hit me in the forehead with his left arm, not a fist, just a wild backhand.

I managed to pull to my feet. I started to drag him toward the door when he went off balance and spun around on his knees to the floor, face first. I jerked back toward the open doorway where I thought I might take the Buck knife to him and get him away from the furniture, but my .38 Special slipped out from my waistband, and it slid to the plywood floor. He lunged for the pistol, stretching and straining, grunting like a man aware of mortality and death.

"You no-good bastard," I hollered, pulling him with both hands at his right arm. From his knees, the man whipped me around into the doorjamb and the wood splintered in a loud crash.

All of a sudden Moxley looked at me with peaceful eyes, a faint grin on his face, his body still tall from the knees up. "You pissant. What do you think you're doing here?" He laughed deep into his belly, kneeling on the floor.

I realized this wouldn't be a citizen's arrest and that I wasn't in control. I released my grip on his arm and unsheathed the Buck and went for his chest with all my strength, but Moxley slung me past him and I was out flat on my back in a second, the air emptied from my lungs, the knife gone God only knows where.

"You little Tadlock piece of shit. You ain't liked it when I runned the girl off the road, did ye? You ain't liked the dead old man. You got more'n you could take."

He was breathing hard, laughing, mocking, and I was trying to apprise myself of some way of escape, trying to get my air but none was present; my head was in a great torment like a brain concussion. But my damned wrist was irrevocably attached to the man.

He stood, dragging me a few feet. Then he cocked the .38 and stuck it to my head.

"Little Tadlock's going to learn him a lesson yet." He started to drag me again to the door, out toward the porch to the sound of legions of dogs and roosters. "I'll feed your shitty ass to Saul."

As he dragged me by my wrist, I remembered the big pistol, it gouging my back as he pulled. I worked it from my lower back as he passed through the doorway and I pulled back on the hammer and pointed it for the first shot. Before I could press the trigger he fired at me, and thank God he missed, but the powder and fire half-blinded me.

My hand bucked and I sailed one into him good. I swear there was a sound of flesh wrapping around the big bullet. Then I heard wailing sounds above me. It sounded like demons leaving his body, haunting yowls and cries of some distant world. Before I could enjoy victory, a shot entered my left shoulder and I thought I was truly dead, the meat splattering against my face.

Moxley towered and I pulled the trigger again and again. The smell of cordite coalesced into a fog of pain. He danced to the bullets and fell halfway down the steps, his collapse dragging me to the edge of the porch. I'd fired seven times before the chamber flew open.

Blood drained from my shoulder where I lay on my back, staring at the hand attached to my wrist, wondering how in the world I ever got there.

Moxley strangled and shook, blood choking him. Rich blood spewed four feet in the air, across my chest like a water fountain. Spray. Spray. Spray. The bloodline started to play out, growing shorter.

I struggled to my side and began trying to move toward the door, crawl over and call the fire department, but I couldn't move the man chained to my bum shoulder. He wasn't really bleeding anymore; he was dying. I realized Moxley was dead. I finally put down the pistol on the wood floor under the porch light and began digging for the hand-cuff keys, but I couldn't get to them. I couldn't feel them at all. I must have dropped them on the ground in the woods. I stood there looking at the man half on the porch, half off. I kept after the keys, and I dug and dug in my pants, salty water pouring off my chin. I finally gave up and started to drag Moxley's corpse off the steps and back into the filthy house, unaware if I could move him the distance to the phone.

The monster's face was shattered and his beard was like a bale of cotton drenched in red blood. A hole the size of a quarter was open in his throat, and a drip of blood fell steady down the side of his neck, and his blood covered my clothes to such a degree that I couldn't tell how badly I was hemorrhaging myself.

I pulled Moxley toward the threshold of the front door. In one minute I was on the phone with the Mount Olive Fire Department. I thought I might bleed to death myself, bleed down before I could get help, but the firemen were at the place in ten minutes. A volunteer fireman's truck entering the dog-infested yard. The pair of cuffs were still on me and Moxley when the fireman arrived. From the way they acted, it was as if these local men knew they'd one day find Moxley killed dead, and they seemed to have no concern about it. They removed the cuff off my wrist with red bolt cutters. I don't know if they ever took the cuff off of Moxley. They loaded me into an ambulance for transport.

CHAPTER 32

I lay in the bed for two days. I wasn't completely conscious at first, and that was good because of the gunshot wound, and because of Uncle Red's death. Finally, when I did come out of the haze, I was so drugged I was slow getting my mind back. I was in a regular room at Ninth Ward Hospital, and I fought the pain more and more; hellhounds of pain that only subsided with doses of Demerol. I'd come to and see Uncle Red's face and well up with despair. My left shoulder was damaged, but at least the internal bleeding had stopped, the doctors said.

Penny was admitted to the hospital and was released the same night. I was pleased about that.

They hadn't yet charged me with murder or manslaughter, but Roberts's man Felix Dufrene had questioned me while I lay in bed, and the D.A. was stirring the waters, poking around in the muck of Moxley's death. The newspaper in Pickleyville ran two brief articles about the shooting. Ellis told me not to speak of the event to anyone unless he was present. Period. He was there when Dufrene showed up. Afterward, Ellis explained that they were throwing underhand pitches at a very slow speed, obvious to him that the sheriff wanted me out of the limelight, Ellis said.

Someone cracked the door the third night I was there, and I figured it was Penny or Terry the nurse. The door opened all the way, and I saw that it wasn't hospital staff. The TV was on but muted and there was a strange blue-green glow in the room.

"Jesse Tadlock." I heard a woman's voice at the door. I didn't recognize the voice. "It's Nokomis Moxley."

"Come in." I opened my eyes wide. The woman wore a blue skirt and blouse that contoured around her thick breasts. She came right near to where I lay. She stood expressionless.

"I come to see you. I knowed he put you in here. I knowed you had to do what you done, and I was glad of it. I knowed he near-about kilt a uncle of your'n and sure enough kilt another." She continued to stand over me.

"Have a seat," I offered, and I immediately felt bad about it. Then I chuckled, perhaps for the first time since the night Uncle Red was electrocuted. I don't know why I laughed.

"I spect I will. She pulled the chair over and sat. I pushed the bed's button and raised myself up to a sitting position. I slipped my hand on the emergency call for the nurses' station, unsure of what Nokomis had in mind.

"When I was a youngun, seventeen years old, I was pure. Twenty years ago. But Cotton was mean to me and to our little boy that drowned in a fishpond when he was three. Him and Cotton together was in the pond. It weren't never crystal clear to me what happened; he was probably kilt, our son. Cotton had a power over me. I weren't able to leave him. It were the devils. He had a devil inside him that sometimes sat on his shoulder like a crow on a fence post."

I wasn't sure where this was going. I listened and kept my finger on the red button attached to the bed rail to call a nurse if necessary.

"I'm a Christian woman," she said.

"Yes ma'am."

"I knowed you'd believe me for that. I had no choice. He had started with our girl. She's tiny for a ten-year-old. He was selling pictures of her to men when he was on the road with the bulldogs. Lord, I told Cotton he could beat me, sell pictures of me, and do what vile things he wants, shoot me, but no, he could not touch Marleah.

"That baby bled for days. He said if I called the law he'd hear it before I got the phone hung up. He told me to pour kerosene down into her privates. I wouldn't. So, he did it hisself. He threatened to stick a match to it. The bawling like you never heard, that girl's bawling.

"I done decided it had to stop. If he touched her again I'd stop him for good. I'd kill him with one of his guns. Then Marleah wouldn't have nobody to raise her. She'd be alone. I had to go to the law on him. I had to go to the hospital, and I had to tell it to the welfare police the night you come over to kill him."

The woman kept talking, telling me how darkened her own heart had become, how she needed forgiveness. How she prayed day and night for somebody to come and end the cruelty. She said things to me I didn't want to hear about Moxley. Then she said something that gave me chills.

"When they told me Cotton was dead, that you was hurt and up in the middle of it, I knew God hisself come to save us. I knowed God was with you and He answered our prayers."

"Well, I just hope they don't send me to jail," I said.

"I ain't supposed to tell you this, but I got a appointment at the Ruthberry courthouse for a grand jury. Three days from now at ten in the morning, and I'm going to go tell them that my husband had us as slaves and that he was a evil man. He was going to kill you and us if you'd not done what you did."

I nodded my head.

"I saw the law already, and I talked to Sheriff Haltom hisself, Cotton's half-brother, if you don't already know. They asked me questions and I told all of them that I seen the checks from his office where Cotton was on the payroll, and I'd be on Channel 2 News over in Baton Rouge City if something bad come of you."

She sat there and I looked into the woman's face, thinking, *much obliged*, but I said nothing.

The woman went on, "After the funeral service me and Marleah went out into the yard with one of Cotton's rifles and a box of shells. People was already calling, wanting to buy the dogs and roosters for big money. We took the van. Do you know what I did?"

"No ma'am."

"I shot every dog in the head with a .22 bullet. Marleah helped me load them. When we got to Saul, his big stud dog, I just hooked a rope to his collar and dragged him with the van to the trash hole dug in the back of the place. He was heavy. They was a mound of dogs' bodies, and we threw them in the trash hole. We piled them up like stove wood one atop the other. Twenty dead bulldogs in a pile, and then we pushed and dragged Saul and rolled him down the bank with the rest. After getting that stud dog on the pile, I poured a five-gallon can of kerosene on them bulldogs. I lit it and watched flames rise into the air. Let them burn to high heaven, every last one of them.

"You saved me and Marleah. Cotton raping and killing the innocent. Killing and raping is all what he did. It was the only thing the man was good for."

There really wasn't a proper way to respond. I didn't know what to say. I just looked at her. "What are y'all going to do now?" I asked.

"Shelby Dunn can have the place. He's going to pay cash money. I'm moving Marleah and me to my sister's over in Theodore, Alabama. She has a cake shop at her house and I'm going to go help her out. Just having a place somewhere and getting away from here is all that matters to us right now."

When she turned to leave, she said that she was sorry for what happened to me and my kin.

I watched her shut the door. Soon, perhaps a minute later, I slept like a baby, the best sleep in months, the sleep of knowing the truth.

The time in the hospital lasted one more day and night at Ninth Ward. I still wasn't charged with any crimes on the Moxley affair, but I was hearing more about the grand jury. Then Haltom Roberts came and arrested me, a manslaughter arrest, not murder, and I bonded out in two hours.

CHAPTER 33

Ellis milled around the courthouse, complimenting the secretaries' hair, shaking hands with the Clerk of Court, spreading goodwill from janitor to judge, hoping to pick something up below the radar in the Baxter Parish Courthouse, hoping for some sense of where the bomb might fall, hoping to minimize the damages.

I was the target, and this was my first and only arrest, but I wasn't at the courthouse alone. Twenty-seven of my kin were present that day, men in overalls, men in worn blue suits with clip-on ties, women in long dresses or in tight blue jeans. It looked like a redneck mob, and they might behave like a mob if provoked.

We sat in the musty hallway, maybe fifty feet from the jury room. Sheriff Haltom Roberts and his chief deputy entered the back of the courthouse like molten shadows wearing polished black cowboy boots and felt hats, like outlaws with silver badges pinned to their chests. The two men's faces were cut deep with the look of annoyance brought on by power and small-town privilege, the certainty of prevailing against any challenge. From where I sat they looked like gods at twilight.

If it were not for the wound healing in my shoulder, my arm in a sling, I might have thought the whole thing was some kind of bad dream. I was still shook up, but what I did, I'd do again. Terror and fear were absent from me in this place of so-called justice. I guess I had a right to be worried, but mostly I felt an abiding concern that transcends both fear and worry, the kind of questions that a man has when he wonders if the truth will prevail in a crooked world.

Fresh cigarette smoke crossed before my eyes from Aunt Cat's Pall Mall. She sat on the pew beside me at my left in the hallway, as the two men were coming toward us. Penny squeezed my right arm when she saw that my eyes had found the men.

"There's the law," Aunt Cat said, kind of looking past me as the sheriff opened the wooden door to the grand jury room, his chief deputy standing outside the door like a sentry.

My throat was dry and I could feel disgust welling up in my stomach. "I need some air," I told the women. I got up and left Penny and Aunt Cat sitting on the church pew, passed a bailiff who was escorting a lanky prisoner wearing stripes. I stepped toward the porch ready for some fresh air.

At the wide glass doors a woman brushed my shoulder, no expression on her face, a hard woman's features sharp with bone. It was Nokomis Moxley. Before I could even speak, she turned around, the glass door between us, and she smiled an unknowable smile, a woman with an unknowable soul. As the door closed, the glare from the concrete floor took her from my sight, and I longed to know what she would do behind the closed doors of the grand jury.

We stayed there all day at the courthouse. It was Thursday. The sheriff's time was the longest, one hour. There were people in and out. Nokomis stayed twenty-two minutes to be exact. The McLin deputy was there, the Hart boy. None spoke to me as I sat on the bench between Penny and Aunt Cat. Aunt Latrice was in too bad a shape to come. Carlin was there, in my defense, his face greasy with salve, his stitches ready to be removed.

The D.A. didn't call me. I wanted to tell the tale, but Ellis said he was glad I didn't get called. Just lots of sitting and waiting. I smoked a half dozen of Penny's menthols.

The next day, Ellis called me at Penny's house. He said the D.A. wouldn't go to trial. He said the grand jury proceedings were sealed and that the matter was closed. As easy as it is to get a grand jury to send someone to trial, Ellis told me, Haltom Roberts must have squashed it.

When I put down the phone I was a new man.

EPILOGUE

Six weeks ago I killed a man. I killed but did not murder.

My arm is out of the sling, but it's stiff. Almost every afternoon I drive over to Taylor Hill Cemetery where I rest under the oak trees and look at Mama's mound of clay in front of the flagpole, a few feet over from where my daddy is buried. I sometimes remove rocks and leaves from Uncle Red's grave. I might spend a half hour there in the cemetery.

This day is no different. The dirt is starting to settle on the graves. I can't speak or shed tears out here. I pull up a plastic chair left out in the graveyard and sit a spell in front of the mound of earth and look at the spot where my uncle lives. My truck is parked there at the grassed-over cemetery lane.

Today I am digging a little footer to make a concrete border around Uncle Red's grave, the place where Aunt Latrice will one day be buried too. I feel an itch beneath the last bandage. I let the shovel stand stuck in the clay dirt. I ease my shirt back from the left shoulder. I push aside the dressing and see the stitches, the proud red scar. It's the length of a man's finger. The bullet didn't break the bone, thank God, but it screwed up the shoulder bad enough. I have a hard time removing the soil from the long footer where the concrete will be poured. My shoulder isn't strong yet.

Aunt Latrice tried to hold the funeral for me but she couldn't. They had to plant him in the ground. It hurt me more than anything to know that I couldn't be a part of his hand-dug hole in the earth. The grave digging was a tradition, not a necessity. I regretted missing this piece of family tradition and history. One thing I did do for him, and I don't regret it, though I am not proud of it, is to send Cotton Moxley to his own grave. In this way perhaps I made up for not digging Uncle Red's hole. Killing Moxley was what he really wanted me to do. It needed to be done for the peace of Baxter Parish.

The fire marshal never came up with a reason or cause for the electric box not to be grounded, though I know who caused it. Ellis knows and the rest of the family suspects it was Moxley. Penny knows who ran her off the road. I know it was Moxley who cooked Uncle Red and tried to kill Penny.

I can still see his face when I put the cuff on him. I was a nuisance. I was a joke to him, a little pain in the ass. I can still see him taking the slugs.

My favorite uncle's headstone is in a line down from all the other Tadlocks. They delivered the stone last week. The headstone is a wide piece of granite with his name, date of birth, and date of death carved in it. Aunt Latrice's name is there too and date of birth. The date of death is still a smooth, flat place on the granite.

Dozens of my people's remains are here, or what we think are their remains, the souls of Tadlocks and the souls of Nards.

One day mine will be here, too. It will read:

JESSE ERNEST TADLOCK

BORN JANUARY 6, 1959

DIED

A stonemason will gladly fill in the blank space with a month and day, four numbers for the year.

Without jockeying for position and without really knowing why, I became the family leader when Uncle Red died. I took his place in the order of things.

It all changed at a little party they threw for me after the grand jury let me go. We had a store-bought cake with coconut icing. It read, "WELCOME HOME JESSE."

Carlin quieted the crowd by tapping his fork against his tea glass. "This man right here saved our whole family. Y'all do well to pay attention to him. Y'all listen to him when he talks. Take heed of what he says."

Nobody said a word. Penny squeezed my hand. Like that it happened. I was anointed the family leader with just those few words.

Maybe it's because Balem Moxley couldn't kill me, and yet he killed Uncle Red. In Baxter Parish, survival is the chief virtue, the only thing that really matters. If any man has ever tried to kill another man, Moxley did me. I know he planned to electrocute me, not my uncle. I was not without malice myself, and I hated Moxley and wished his death as he wished mine. I wanted him dead like one of his dogs. I guess everybody at the family gathering could see it. They could see me standing there alive, too.

I own the land and the old farmhouse up in Mount Olive. But I'm planning on selling it and buying Aunt Latrice's rent house. I'm living there in Packwood Corners now. I sold every tree up in Mount Olive except for the pecans, and am living off the money, paying bills. I didn't get the job at Tidwell's on account of the hospital stay and my injuries. I'm trying to recuperate.

Pretty soon I'll start school at Baxter State, live low on the hog, draw the college benefits from the service, maybe work a little cash business using Uncle Red's boat, sell fish to the professors and staff who work out there at the junior college. I'm going to start getting the basic courses out the way, maybe try accounting.

I like the way accountants are always able to balance the books or figure out exactly where a dollar went. I kind of like a stable universe. That's just what I'm looking for the rest of my life. I like predictability and I've always been good with numbers.

This morning I drove out to Bayou Square Mall. I looked at rings, put engagement rings on my pinky finger to see how they shine. I got it in my truck, three-quarter carat. I like the roundness of that diamond, the circle of it. I bet it's going to glisten on Penny's hand in a couple of days when I give it to her. I believe I'm going to marry Penny Nesom if she'll have me.

At this point, I hope to stay in Packwood Corners, to do my best to live right around home. I'll not shy away from any fights. I'll stare down the trouble in this place, just take things as they come.

This is how it all turns out. I'm a free man. The whole crazy business and I'm still free. Wounded, but free.

When folks ask me about life after the Army, when they ask about coming back home, I tell them it's like returning to a fallen paradise. That's what it's like living in Baxter Parish again.

What sense would it all make if it wasn't a true story? Who would ever believe it if it wasn't true as dirt?

ACKNOWLEDGMENTS

I am a thirty-four-year-old who spent three years in ninth grade, and then dropped out of high school. Sixteen years ago I took my GED and went to college. Now, the master's degree finished, I am an assistant professor and, I hope, a novelist. This journey did not happen by my own design, nor did it occur without good teaching, most of it at Southeastern Louisiana University in Hammond.

I wish to thank novelist Tim Gautreaux for trying to teach me about writing fiction. I also thank my readers and research consultants: My wife Kristy, Nikki Barranger, Ali Meyer, Callie Foreman, Staci and Jason Parrie, Laverne Simoneaux, Ladonna Guillot, Beth Stahr, Karen Williams, Harry B. Sherman, Randy Davis, Darren Barnes, Lamar Wascom, Kyle Bruhl, Daddy, Sheila and Gabe Morley, Carol Chester, Carl and Carolyn Higginbotham, Lee Rozelle, David Campbell, Harrell Weathersby, and Stephen Doiron, to name a few. Thanks goes to my bosses, J.B. Hill and Eric Johnson, for humoring me when I catch the story-telling spirit. Much obliged to Inman Majors and James Fox-Smith, two fine editors who were both kind enough to publish the seed story for this novel in their respective magazines.

Bev Marshall—kin from Mississippi—thanks for your encouragement. You mentioned Sonny Brewer at the family reunion up at Mars Hill a couple of years ago, and this changed the direction of my writing life.

To Sonny, Alabama Don of the Southern Literary Mafia: no one is more responsible for breathing life into my writing vocation than you.

You simply said to get on with it and write the story.

Thanks to Fairhope writers and readers: Martin Lanaux, Jim Gilbert, Joe Formichella, Frank Turner Hollon, Suzanne Hudson, and Rick Bragg. Y'all make me feel like writing is the most important human endeavor.

I owe thanks to my parents for bringing me up in this rich and dangerous parish and for providing me with a host of stories from which my fiction can grow.

The Louisiana Division of the Arts gave me a literature grant in 2003, my first award for writing, and I am grateful for the kind support.

To the gang at MacAdam/Cage, David Poindexter, Pat Walsh, Scott Allen, Tasha Kepler, and the others: Thanks for taking me on as one of your authors.

And finally, special thanks goes to Kristy. Thank you for the patience. Few wives would allow a brand new husband to meet with his future editor while on the honeymoon. I love you and cherish our lives together, now and forever.